JUMP THROUGH FIRE

Harem of Freaks Book 4

CRYSTAL ASH

PROLOGUE

Fire. So much fire.

I always smelled it before I saw it. Before the humans prodded me out of my tiny cage with their electric sticks just far enough to snap a chain on the degrading collar around my neck so they could drag me the rest of the way out.

What an awful, sickening, burning smell. Years ago, I enjoyed the smoky warmth of a wood burning fire. We never cooked our food, of course, but the bonfire was the center of our community. Grandparents told stories while children laughed and ran circles around the massive flames.

But this fire was all gasoline and chemicals. I prayed the fumes would give cancer to these wretched humans.

"Keep moving, stupid cat."

They zapped my flanks with the cattle prods to keep my back legs moving, but I barely felt the shocks anymore. Even the feeling in my paws had all but disappeared due to the multiple burns. But I'd be damned if I made this easy on them. I was still a 500-pound animal, and I'd make sure they'd feel every ounce of my weight as they dragged me closer to that awful smell.

At first, I thought if I went along with their demands like a well-trained pet, they'd stop shocking me. Maybe treat my burns. Or give me a decent meal for once.

I gave up on that hope years ago. If they were going to torture me regardless, pissing them off would give me a tiny amount of satisfaction.

Two of them pushed open a set of heavy wooden doors, leading me out into the ring. My usual getup, a tiny stool set in front of three fiery metal hoops, waited for me in the center.

Oohs and *ahhs* rose up from the crowd of humans in the stands surrounding us. Hundreds of different scents assaulted my nose underneath the sickly sweetness of the gasoline. That could only mean a packed house tonight.

My handlers discreetly prodded me up to the tiny stool —they wouldn't want to be reported for animal cruelty now—where I sat awkwardly on my haunches. Heat assaulted my face from the fiery hoops. The flames looked bigger and brighter tonight. No doubt the ringmaster ordered it as a punishment for maiming his assistant last night.

He stood in the center of the pit, in his stupid red tail-coat and top hat, talking me up to the crowd. I watched him through the flames like looking at prey through tall grass. A sudden thought occurred to me.

No. You will be too far gone if you do such a thing. Your soul will never be saved.

But what hope did I have left? The shaman hadn't

reached out to me in over a day. I wasn't even sure if she was real or a hallucination at this point.

The ringmaster gestured to me as he completed his speech for the audience, turning his head to meet my eyes. Those cold, dead eyes that showed no remorse as he and his people abused, tortured, and starved me, plus who knew how many others like me.

Part of me thought I should have gone with Razvan all those years ago, but if it weren't me here, it would only be another shifter as a dancing puppet for these cruel masters. The ringmaster's eyes narrowed at me through the circles of flames, a warning to obey.

A roar from deep in my chest was my answer, my teeth on full display and my human head-sized paw swiping through the air. I made my decision. In the grand scheme of things, I was already dead.

I'd never see *svarga* after this life, but I was at peace with that. After all of my impure thoughts while trapped in this Hell, taking one human with me wouldn't be the worst thing. Maybe the next shifters' lives would be a bit easier until they found a new ringmaster.

I lowered my paw to the edge of the stool and lifted my rear end, coiled and poised to take my jump. So much fire. I fought back the nausea and the fear whispering at my instincts. This would be my last jump for these bastards and I had to make it count.

I focused on my prey, stilled my breath and my body, then leaped.

Flames licked painfully at my skin, singeing the fur on both sides of my flanks. I tucked my front paws as close to my body as I could. Only when I passed through the final hoop did I extend my claws.

Gasps of awe turned to screams of horror as I shredded through the ringmaster's coat. It was almost comical how his eyes bulged too late to realize what was happening. He didn't even have a chance to scream as my teeth sank into his throat.

Oh, a delicious, raw, fresh kill...

The sting in my shoulder only made me clamp down harder, tearing into the human's soft, pliable body with urgency.

So much blood. Delicious, sweet, hot flesh...

More stings pelted my body and my paws became heavy, so incredibly heavy. I smiled inwardly as the tranquilizers began circulating through my system, admiring the work I made of the former ringmaster. Now *that* wouldn't be an open-casket funeral.

I laid my head down and allowed the darkness to swallow me up. If I had any luck left at all, I would never wake up.

MELODY

I almost couldn't reach the door fast enough. The contents of last night's dinner roiled like a stormy sea up through my throat and nose, then spilled all over the concrete of the parking lot just outside of the trailer.

My stomach emptied itself, and then I dry-heaved through more coughs and gasps.

"Baby, please," Connor cried dramatically from inside the RV, "for the love of all that is holy, do not tell me you are pregnant."

"Asshole," I wheezed, spitting on the ground as I tried desperately to clear my throat.

"Here, *steluţa*." A tattooed hand held out a water bottle to me, which I accepted and pulled from greedily. "Is McDonald's not agreeing with you?"

"It's not that," I gasped after draining half of the bottle. "Another vision. This one was... really, really gruesome."

"Here. Let's get you cleaned up, then you can tell us

about it." Razvan rubbed my back soothingly. Since the moment we left Crying Falls, he seemed to have replaced Hunter as the sweetheart of the group. When he wasn't manhandling me and whispering all the dirty things he wanted to do to me, that was.

The tattooed dragon shifter led me, still weak and shaky, back inside to the tiny bathroom of the RV. After I brushed my teeth and washed my face, I felt slightly more human.

"What did you see?" Raz's gray eyes were wide with concern as he sat me on the bed next to Connor, who was still naked under the sheet.

"I saw through the eyes of the big predator again, the one we're getting closer to," I explained. "This time, he attacked the ringmaster. I'm pretty sure he killed him. I —" my hand flew to my throat. "I felt and tasted *everything*. The softness of his flesh, the warm stickiness of his blood. And I—no, the shifter, enjoyed it. He hadn't killed any prey in so long, and it was such a rush. But he..." My hand lowered to my lap as I recalled that feeling, the finality of it. "He had given up on escaping. He did it because he didn't expect to live much longer. Fuck, if they kill him—"

"Shh, babe." Connor sat up immediately and cradled my head to his chest. "Do not blame yourself. You can't save everyone."

"Then what the fuck is the point of me being a shaman?" I cried out in frustration. "They need me and I can't figure it out. I keep screwing up."

"You're not screwing up," Raz insisted, squeezing my knee. "You're learning. You're doing what you can."

"Eww, what's this?"

"Looks like vomit. Watch out, don't step in it."

The voices from outside the trailer indicated Hunter and the pups had returned from their early morning run, and the atmosphere immediately changed. Hunter didn't spare us a glance as he entered the trailer and took his place in the driver's seat.

Meanwhile, Raz and Connor glared daggers at his back. A full day on the road out of Crying Falls and he barely spoke a word to anyone but his kids. Oblivious to the tension, Roo and Rinna playfully wrestled on the floor.

"Don't worry, babe," Connor murmured with a kiss to my cheek. "About anything. We'll find your shifter and address the wolf in the room."

Hunter's canine hearing almost surely allowed him to hear Connor, although he made no sign that he did.

"Ready to hit the road, guys?" Connor announced in a louder voice.

"Yeah!" the kids declared in unison. Silence from the driver's seat.

Raz let out a frustrated growl as he squeezed my thigh. "Ride with me, *steluța*," he insisted.

I nodded, eager to be out of range of Hunter's cold shoulder. It was awkward enough on the drive yesterday. I didn't know if I'd be able to handle one more day without exploding.

"Now, don't get up to anything frisky, you two," Connor winked. "Eyes on the road, Raz."

"Shit, it's hard enough to focus with her just sitting next to me," Raz grinned as he pulled me to my feet, planted a kiss on me, and walked me out of the trailer, careful to sidestep over my vomit on the ground.

He turned to me the moment we shut the doors of his

truck cab. "Con's gonna get to the bottom of whatever's eating wolf-boy's tail, I just know it."

"I know he will," I sighed, buckling my seatbelt. "I'm just afraid of what the answer will be."

"Don't be." He turned the ignition and the massive V8 engine roared to life. "I promise it has everything to do with him and nothing to do with you."

"You don't know that for sure," I said as we pulled out of the parking lot. My eyes flicked to the rearview mirror, where I saw Hunter maneuver the RV to follow us with Connor in the passenger seat.

"Yes, I do," my sexy dragon insisted.

"Change of subject, please." I looked out the window to the stretch of dense trees across the parking lot. We stopped for the night at a Wal-Mart out near the sticks for food and other essentials, like enough privacy for the shifters to shift. Raz didn't want to risk being seen even at night, so he slunk around in the woods in dragon form for a few hours last night. Hunter preferred early morning runs with the kids in wolf form. They caught their breakfast that way, too.

"How close are we to your old home?" Raz asked after a moment of hesitation.

I grimaced. Not the subject change I exactly wanted. Our ultimate destination was Eddison, Georgia, where Connor would be fitted with new leg prosthetics and be treated for the pain that landed him in the hospital back in Crying Falls. And if my gut was right, we'd be near this shifter whose eyes I kept seeing through in my dreams lately.

Unfortunately, our journey would also take us straight through Waterford, Alabama. Trailer trash central and my home sweet home. If a rundown trailer with an alcoholic mother and too many siblings to care for could ever be considered a home.

"Not nearly far enough," I muttered in reply.

Razvan chuckled. "You don't wish to see them? Not even at all?"

"My mom probably hasn't even noticed I'm gone yet," I scoffed. "Or if she has, it's only because her live-in maid and cook has disappeared." A question popped into my head as I drummed my fingertips on the window. "Do you ever wish to see your family again? Even after what they did to you?"

Raz inhaled a sharp breath as he mulled over his answer. He was the first dragon shifter born in his family for centuries, as the shifting gene had gone dormant. His family was so far removed from his dragon heritage, they regarded his shifting as a curse on their family. To absolve themselves of the so-called curse, they sold their son into the local circus.

"Not my parents," he answered, his voice gruff. "I would only want to see my younger siblings, to see if they exhibit any of the traits that I did. I'd want them to know they could find me, if they ever wanted that."

"When did you last talk to them?" I asked.

"Over five years ago," he sighed. "Right before I was shipped over here from Romania as cargo. I didn't even have an ID or a passport." He shot me a wry smile. "If I had come here voluntarily, I would have been an illegal immigrant."

"Oh no, not one of those!" I teased.

"Yes. It's easier to come over here as an exotic pet, it turns out. But anyway," his smile dropped as he turned the truck onto the freeway. "I think of them often and wish I could contact them. Every day that passes feels like it's too late to reach out. So I say, don't wait until five years have suddenly gone by, *steluţa*."

"You're right," I breathed. "I just wish I had something more to give them. Some money or a place to stay away from her."

"You'll give them hope," he said, placing his hand on my knee. "They'll see you living your own life and answering to no one. They'll remember that. Even if they can't leave right away, they'll make plans and count down the days until they can."

I didn't answer him right away. I just squeezed his fingers around my knee, tracing the dots and lines of the tattoos on his hand. Getting away from that place had been the primary goal of my life. The thought of going back only filled me with dread.

Guilt also ate at me. I left them vulnerable to *her*. All my life, I'd been the shield between them and the wastes of life she brought home. I left to take care of myself, but no one else could defend them.

With a resigned sigh, I focused on the moving road ahead of us.

"I guess we're taking a detour, then."

CONNOR

"Alright, dude. Spill it."

Hunter's eyebrow twitched, but aside from that, he gave no indication that he heard me.

"Hunter, bro," I turned in the passenger seat to face him. "I know you didn't become deaf overnight. It's just us now. What the fuck is going on?"

"Nothing," the wolf shifter muttered.

"We both know that's bullshit. Try again."

He let out a heavy sigh, his eyes flicking to the rearview mirror to double-check that his children were indeed asleep.

"You can't tell Mel what I'm about to tell you. I mean, she deserves to know but I haven't processed it all yet."

"Sure, tell her in your own time. As long as you nut the fuck up, apologize for being a dick, and stop acting like one." I waved my hand between him and me as he drove. "And for the record, I can't believe *I'm* the one telling you to stop being a dick."

"I know," he snorted with a dry laugh. "What a role reversal, huh?"

"Spit it out, wolf-boy. I'm frothing at the mouth here."

He glanced over his shoulder once again to make sure the kids were asleep.

"After Mel and I were... together, with Razvan," he began in a voice so low I almost couldn't hear, "I went to check on the kids and spend some time with them. Rinna asked me something."

"Yeah?"

He swallowed and inhaled deeply. "She asked me if Mel would become their mom."

I rubbed my jaw. "And what did you say?"

"I don't even remember what lame excuse I said," he shook his head. "But I wanted so badly to say yes. And just the fact that I *wanted* to say that, just made me feel all guilty and pissed off."

"Why's that?" I probed, feeling like a damn therapist.

"Because my mate was her mother," he said with a soft growl. "Yes, she's dead. Yes, she wasn't perfect. But she was a wolf, a good she-wolf on her way to becoming alpha. And I can't shake the idea that's been instilled into me since I was a kid."

"And that is?"

His golden eyes flickered to me before returning to the road. "Pups need to be raised by their own kind. I can either be a single parent or I can find another pack and take another wolf for a mate. What I can't have is a shifter of another species, and especially not a human, raise my kids."

"Okay," I answered, mulling around this new information in my mind. "And this is really bothering you because you *do* want Mel in your life? As a possible mother figure to them?"

"Yes," he breathed, his fingers tightening his grip on the steering wheel. "I'm falling for her, Con. I'm falling hard."

"Obviously," I quipped. "Both of you are gaga over her. I mean, my advice would be just to get the fuck over your wolf pride hangups. The pups love her and she adores them. She may not be a shifter, but she understands you guys better than any normal human. Even if she can't teach them your wolf stuff, she can contribute to the human aspect."

"That's not all that's weighing on me." He gritted his teeth, his knuckles growing white on the steering. "In fact, that's not even the main reason I can't bring myself to talk or look at her."

I stared at him, taken aback. "What is it, Hunt?"

A long silence stretched between us. The stress and struggle to speak the words were visible on his face as I watched him.

"I am also kind of interested in another person."

"Hunter," I barked, sitting up straight. "You need to tell her this, ASAP. It's not fair to her. I'm talking the moment we stop for gas, you need to march your ass over there and tell her or I will."

"I know, but Con, it's not that simp—"

"I don't give a fuck, dude! Yes, our situation is unusual and I get that. But Mel is not anyone's side piece and I will *not* let her be treated like one."

"It's not really—"

"I don't care how you try to justify it, that's just how it is. You gotta make a choice, dude. You're either all in with Mel and us or you're not."

"But that's the thing," he said with a small shake of his head.

I barely heard him. The moment he said another person, my temper started to rise and I would have reached over and slugged him if he wasn't driving. He saw how distraught Mel was when my ex came to see me in the hospital. He *knew* how torn up she was! How could he comfort her from *that*, encourage her to come back to me, and still have a wandering eye for another woman?

"Let me guess," I spat bitterly. "You met a lady wolf shifter who is a perfect mother figure for your kids on paper, but you don't know her as well as Mel. Is that why this is so hard for you?"

"No!" he barked, glaring at me from the corner of his eye. "A female wolf wouldn't even make me look twice standing next to her."

"So what the fuck makes this person so special?"

"Look, I'll talk to her." His voice turned pleading. "The moment we stop, I'll man up and explain myself. Just please let me tell her myself. I don't want any information to get twisted."

"Hunter," I rubbed my temples. "I don't even know where you're going with this anymore. Get what twisted? The fact that you're falling for another woman?"

"It's not another woman!" he shouted before quickly glancing over his shoulder at his kids, who remained fast asleep.

I could only stare at him, dumbfounded. That was not what I was expecting.

"Hunter?"

"It's Razvan," he sighed.

3

MELODY

We pulled into a gas station a few hours later, when the sun was high and sweltering. I pulled my legs off of Razvan's lap and swung them around to exit the passenger side. The moment I stepped out of the cool, air-conditioned cab, my thighs and breasts prickled from the sweat forming between them.

Damn, I wondered if the guys would be up for staying in a shitty motel tonight instead of our vehicles. Or maybe we could sneak into one with a pool.

"What're you hungry for, *steluţa?*" Raz asked as he inserted the fuel pump into his car.

"Dragon," I purred, running my arm around his back and up his chest while I laid my head on his back. I couldn't help myself, I was so damn smitten with him.

"Don't tempt me," he chuckled, wrapping his fingers around mine and bringing them to his lips. "How about actual food?"

"Just a sandwich is fine," I told him as he turned to face me. "With no mayo if you can find one."

"And a side of dragon for dessert?" he grinned, stepping forward until my back met the smooth exterior of his car.

Why did I love it so much when he pinned me like this? He took the opportunity at every stop and it turned me to jello every time.

"Yes," I answered, my voice already getting breathy. "Piping hot, please."

He lowered a kiss to my mouth with a predatory growl, his upper body leaning in and pressing me hard against his truck. We must have kissed hundreds of times at this point, so much that my mouth memorized his. But when that split tongue flicked against mine playfully, it stole my breath away like the first time all over again.

"We'll have to kick those two out of the RV tonight," he voiced huskily as we untangled. "I want you in a proper bed."

"Why does that mean we have to kick them out?" I asked innocently, although my smile was anything but.

"You're so naughty and I love it," he said with a possessive squeeze of my waist. "Conner is always welcome to join but I don't want Mr. Party Pooper over there killing my mood."

I glanced up toward the RV, which Hunter pulled up to another fuel pump several feet away. He set up Connor's wheelchair just outside the door, and all of us watched as Connor handstanded his way out of the trailer and swung himself into the chair like a gymnast.

"Show off." Raz kissed my forehead before leaving me to head inside the mini-mart. "Sandwich with no mayo coming right up."

"Mel." I barely had time to enjoy the backside view of Raz walking away before a voice called my name. My heart jumped into my throat as I saw Hunter taking his long strides toward me. "Can I talk to you?"

"Um, sure," I answered hesitantly, not bothering to hide my surprise.

It seemed Connor really had gotten through to him. His expression was no longer cold and blank. Rather, the wolf shifter's brow was knitted as if worried. His golden eyes shifted around, never looking right at me. He appeared more tense and nervous than I'd ever seen him before.

I followed him away from the gas pumps, noticing Connor was preoccupied with showing the kids around the outside of the RV. He pointed at the wheels and made elaborate gestures with his hands like he was explaining how cars worked. I couldn't suppress the smile that formed. Even from a distance, I could tell he was a natural teacher.

"What's up?" I asked as casually as I could muster once we were out of earshot, despite my insides roiling like I would throw up again.

"First of all, I'm sorry for being so cold to you," he blurted. "You didn't deserve any of that, and Connor almost literally beat some sense into me. There's no excuse for me acting like that, especially after we got so much closer while he was in the hospital."

I nodded in a tentative acceptance of his apology. But I wasn't ready to let him off the hook yet.

"So what brought on the sudden change?"

He ran a hand through his platinum shoulder-length hair. "A couple of things," he sighed. "The main thing... I didn't want to admit to myself or you, or anyone. I don't know how you feel about it, but regardless, I don't plan on acting on it. So you don't have to worry about me behaving any certain way, but I am dealing with some weird feelings internally."

I blinked, just watching him talk, stammer, and ramble. I'd never seen him so nervous before. Whatever he was talking about clearly bothered him a great deal. He looked like he wanted to tuck his tail between his legs and slink away.

"Hunter, I'm not sure what you're talking about," I admitted.

"Of course you aren't," he muttered, pinching his brow. "I'm just dancing around it because I'm honestly terrified of hurting you with this information."

"Hey." I stepped closer, reaching out to touch him for the first time in days. My hand met his forearm, the contact lighting me up like an electric wire. I missed him, the *old* him. And I desperately wanted to ease the burden of whatever he carried.

"You won't hurt me if you're just honest," I told him. "Even if it's not something I want to hear, I'll appreciate you telling me. What I don't want is you hiding something because you think it'll protect me."

His arm came around me slowly, pulling me in until my cheek rested on his racing heartbeat. He lowered his chin to the top of my head and I heard his deep breaths to steel himself.

"Ever since the three of us were together," he began. "I feel like... I might be into Razvan. Physically. Maybe emotionally, I dunno."

I lifted my head to look up at him. "*That's* what you're

so worried about?"

He nodded, his jaw and lips tense.

"Hunter." His name tasted like dessert on my lip as I slid my arms up to wrap around his neck. "Why would I be upset about that?"

He blinked, the shock setting in. "I dunno. Like I said, I don't know how you feel about... all that. And anyway," he shook his head. "Nothing will ever happen. He's infatuated with you and I won't come between that."

"What if he felt the same way about you?"

His breath hitched in his chest as he stared wide-eyed down at me. His mouth opened as if to ask a question, then quickly changed his mind. "Doesn't matter. We're both here for you. These... feelings don't diminish how I feel for you in the slightest."

"Have you ever felt this way about another man before?"

"No," he answered with a small shake of his head. "I can appreciate a good-looking guy, of course. But seeing him with you? There's something about him that's—never mind." He shook his head even more emphatically. "It doesn't matter. I'll get over it and I won't be a jerk to you anymore. I'm sorry, little fox."

"It's okay," I breathed, my body thrumming with fresh desire at the new fantasies dancing in my head. So I hadn't been entirely wrong when I noticed the connection between Raz and Hunter. But damn, sometimes I hated the small-mindedness of the south.

"Listen." I stood on tiptoes to stretch the full length of my body against his height. "I'm okay with you two being together if you want. I honestly think it's kind of hot."

"Mel," Hunter growled softly, lowering his forehead to

mine. "You wouldn't want to see any of us with another woman, would you?"

"No," I frowned. "I wouldn't like that."

"So if things are truly equal, how is being with another guy any better?" His arms slid around my back. "I could never do that to you."

"Well, it's not just *any* guy," I corrected. "It's Razvan. He's one of us. And if the three of us are together and I'm enjoying both of you, what's wrong with you two enjoying each other in the same moment?"

"I don't know," he murmured, although the growing bulge in his pants told a very different story. "And anyway, we don't know what Raz thinks."

"Want me to talk to him?"

"No!"

Hunter's fingers gripped the sides of my shirt, his brow growing furrowed with anxiety again. "Please don't say anything. I'm nowhere near ready to have that conversation with him. I just didn't want to keep it from you."

"Alright, I won't," I promised, gliding my fingers through his hair. "And I appreciate you telling me. I mean it when I say I'm fine with it. More than fine, even." I paused to lick my lips. "It would make me really happy to see you two together."

"You're serious?" his eyes widened.

"Of course I am!" I lifted my mouth to his, tired of waiting on my wolf for our make-up kiss, and it did not disappoint.

His long arms wrapped around my back and squeezed me against his torso, lifting me up so my toes levitated above the ground. My heart lifted and soared as our mouths molded together, chasing away all the awkwardness of the past few days as we settled back into the way we were.

Voices floating over on the breeze told me Raz and Connor were enjoying the show. I wrapped my legs around Hunter's waist and he grunted through our kisses, binding his arms under my ass to hold me securely against him.

"Was there anything else you wanted to tell me?" I asked when we parted breathlessly.

"No," he smiled. "I'm just so relieved you're okay with knowing this about me."

"I won't betray your confidence," I assured him, sliding my feet back down to the ground. "But you should talk to him. I think he might be more receptive than you think."

He glanced toward Raz, now leaning against the RV while talking to Connor, a plastic grocery bag in one hand.

"I'll think about it," he muttered.

"That's all I can ask for." I reached for his lips on my tip-toes again. "In the meantime, I have a sandwich to eat."

"You do like sandwiches," he grinned wolfishly as we walked back together, our hands swinging between us.

"Stop," I laughed, smacking his arm. "You're just as bad as those two now."

"Kissed and made up, I see," Connor observed when we rejoined them, his eyes glancing between us knowingly.

"Yeah," Hunter cleared his throat. "I owe all of you an apology. I was a complete dick the last couple of days because of my own shit. I didn't mean to take it out on all of you." He squeezed my hand affectionately. "Sorry, guys."

"If Mel forgives you, who are we not to?" Raz rummaged through his bag until he pulled out a deli-wrapped sandwich for me. "No mayo, *steluţa*."

"It's a thing of the past now, bro," Connor added. "Onward and upward. No matter what, you can't unseat me as the moody asshole of the group."

"I'll know not to attempt that again," Hunter laughed, stretching upward and lacing his hands behind his head. My core heated at the sliver of taut belly that peeked from under his shirt. I was dying to make up the proper way, but it would have to wait.

Raz gave me a gentle nudge with his elbow. "Did you still want to do what we talked about?"

No. But we have to do it, anyway.

I nodded and straightened my spine as the other two looked on curiously.

"We'll pass through my old hometown, Waterford, in about two hours," I informed them. "I'd like to stop and check on my siblings, just to let them know I'm alive and okay." I looked at Connor. "Maybe give them a phone number if they need to reach me?"

"My digits are your digits, babe." He blew me a kiss. "You don't even need to ask."

"Thanks." I went to him and sat in his lap, wrapping my arm around his shoulders. "I don't really want to go there, but feel like I have to. I left really suddenly and I want them to know I didn't abandon them."

My Marine wrapped his arms securely around my waist. Here, nothing could reach me. Nothing could hurt me as long as I had them.

"We've got you, babe," he promised. "No matter how many drunk pieces of shit we have to fight in the process."

Raz and Hunter murmured their agreement, casting quick glances at each other before looking away.

4

MELODY

"*This* is where you used to live?"

The question came from Connor, mouth open and agape as we pulled up to the curb right outside the trailer park.

"Yup," I answered. "Home sweet fuckin' home."

"The bus stop I slept at was nicer than this dump." His lip curled in visible disgust.

"Yeah, why do you think I left as soon as I could?" I drummed my fingers on the RV window, remembering that day as clearly as ever. I'd never felt so scared or so free that morning of my eighteenth birthday, when I walked away and never looked back.

It had been barely a month and here I was again. The run-down mobile homes with peeling paint, rusted siding, overgrown yards, and piles of trash looked to be in even worse shape than when I left. Connor's RV was a modest apartment compared to these places. Razvan's setup, with multiple tents for privacy, a king-sized air mattress and even a bathtub, was downright luxurious.

"Which one was yours?" Hunter craned his neck from the driver's seat, looking down the narrow road between the mobile homes.

"Number eight, toward the back." I pointed through Connor's window. "Just on the other side of that woodpile, which has never been used in years. None of the houses have chimneys, so the wood's probably all rotted out and nasty now."

"Hunter should probably be the one to go with you," Connor suggested. "Raz and I might not give the greatest first impression."

I snorted. "It's not like I'm hoping to impress my mom with y'all. Any one of you is ten times whichever man she brought home that week."

"Even so, Hunter's the calmest and most normal-looking out of all of us," Connor chuckled. "You don't need a surly wheelchair-bound Marine and a hot-headed dragon to ruin anything."

I sighed. He had a point. Even if my mom was passed out, my siblings grew to be just as suspicious of strange men as I was. One look at Connor or Raz would send alarm bells ringing and they might not be open to keeping in touch with me. Hunter would be easiest to trust based on first impressions alone.

"Alright," I breathed, moving reluctantly through the door. "Let's get this over with."

"We'll watch from the street," Connor assured. "Just yell if you need anything."

I nodded, blowing a kiss at him before stepping outside with Hunter right on my heels. His fingertips rested on the small of my back and I drew strength from his touch.

Faces peered at us from dirty windows as we walked past the trailers. Some neighbors would surely recognize me and probably already started gossiping about my return with a strange man.

When we stopped in front of the rectangular metal box that looked to be sinking into the soggy ground, Hunter gave my shoulder a gentle squeeze.

"You got this," he whispered with a quick kiss to my forehead. "We're all behind you."

I nodded, taking a quick breath to steel myself, then stepped up to the front door, despite my feet feeling stuck in concrete.

A quick knock on the flimsy, warped plywood, and the door almost immediately cracked open. A blue eye at nearly the same height as me peered through the crack, narrowed in suspicion.

"Jeanie?" I asked. "It's me, Mel."

The door promptly shut, and I heard the lock slide over on the chain.

"Jean!" I knocked again, more insistently, and waited. No answer, so I started pounding at the wood. "Jeanie May, open up!"

"Mel, should we come back?" Hunter asked as he looked around at the nosey neighbors peeking their heads out their own doors, but I ignored him and continued on.

"I'm not coming back here again!" I said through gritted teeth. "This is the *one* time I'm coming back to this shithole, so y'all better—"

The door swung wide open mid-knock, and my fifteen-year-old sister glared at me from across the threshold.

I sucked in a breath. Not even a month went by and

the wide-eyed, strawberry blonde who was closest to me in age suddenly looked to be a decade older.

Jeanie wore a faded, threadbare T-shirt and sweatpants that had been mine at one point, and my older sister's before that. Her hair was piled on her head in a messy bun with dozens of strands poking out like she'd slept with her hair like that. But from the shadows under her eyes, it looked like she barely slept at all.

"Say what you need to say, then go back to wherever you ran off to," Jeanie spat, turning away from the door, leaving it wide open for us.

I stepped inside, Hunter's hand tense on my shoulder as we observed the house where I grew up. Jeanie had been sorting recycling, just like how I taught her to do. In the narrow kitchen, large trash bags were filled to the brim with either aluminum cans, glass bottles, or plastic bottles.

The rest of the trailer hadn't changed much. Piles of unsorted laundry, magazines, children's toys, and old electronics cluttered up the small space, but it was relatively clean. It seemed Jeanie had stepped up to fill my shoes as everyone's caretaker when I left.

"Um, Jean, this is Hunter," I said, waving a hand back toward him. "Hunter, my sister Jeanie May."

"Well met, Jeanie." He offered a friendly smile, carefully ducking under a ceiling light. "Thank you for letting us stop by."

Jeanie rolled her eyes toward me, never pausing as she sorted bottles and cans like a one-woman assembly line. "I just let y'all in so your knocking wouldn't wake them up."

I swallowed. By *them,* she meant Mom and someone else. Sometimes it would mean Audra, our older sister, who followed closely in our mother's drunken, stumbling footsteps. Other times, it meant the guy Mom was seeing at the time.

"Where are the other kids?" I asked.

"School," she answered curtly.

"Oh, good." I breathed a sigh of relief. "I was worried about them not getting up and going without anyone to..." I trailed off, suddenly feeling like a piece of shit for leaving.

"Oh, they missed about a week before I stepped up," Jeanie said. "There was some confusion and shit with you being gone, but shit went back to normal after that."

"I see," I said with a grimace, knowing that our normal wasn't by any means good. And I hated leaving them with that. "Hey, wait. Why aren't *you* in school?"

She stared at me like I sprouted an extra head. "Because *someone* has to take care of shit at home. With you gone, that had to be me. So here I am. Just finished cleaning puke and beer off this floor, now I gotta get this shit sorted and dropped off before I pick up the littles."

"Jean," I pleaded, my teeth biting into my cheek. "You need to stay in school, too."

"I can't, Mel," she shot back. "I can't keep this house from falling apart, *and* go to class, *and* do homework!"

"Honey, I know it's hard." I moved closer to her. "But you have to. You have to get your diploma, then you can walk out of here and apply for jobs. Real jobs. But you have to learn how the world works, how to spend your money and all of that. If you stay here, you'll be trapped."

"So what did you do?" Her eyes shifted from me to Hunter. "Looks like you found a man. Not much different from Mom or Audra, I see."

"Hunter's nothing like them," I hissed, lifting a finger

at her in warning. "My situation's complicated, and it's not perfect, but I am building skills and working toward something, Jean. But I didn't want to ride off into the sunset and leave you and the others behind. That's why I came back, to let you know I'm still here for you guys."

"Yeah?" She lifted her eyebrows. "Look, I'm not mad at you for leaving. I fantasize about it every day, but if you want to help, we need more than your pep talks telling us to stay in school. The kids need new clothes and school supplies. We need new locks on all the doors—"

"The bedroom locks broke again?" Dread filled the pit of my stomach as I raised a hand to my open mouth.

"Oh, Mom broke those fuckers the first night you were gone," Jean remarked casually. "She tore this place up looking for you. It's a wonder there ain't no holes in the walls."

As if right on cue, the sounds of groans, heavy footsteps, and commotion came from down the hall. My heart jumped into my throat and I knew my time here was limited.

"I'll get you locks," I promised. "And stuff for the kids. I can't right away, but I will soon. I swear, Jeanie." I grabbed a pen from the counter and scribbled down Connor's phone number. "You can reach me here with a text or call if you need anything. We're passing through on our way to Georgia, but I can mail you the stuff you need. I can set up a bank account that only you can access."

"Okay." Jeanie's tough exterior seemed to wither away as her eyes darted nervously down the hall. Her voice lowered to a whisper. "Y'all better go. She's been—"

"Jeanie?! Who the fuck're you talking to?"

"No one, Ma!" my sister yelled back.

Hunter's hand closed around my upper arm and he moved to pull me back through the door just as Jeanie stuffed the paper with Connor's number into her shirt. We just reached the door when the shape of my mother emerged from the hall.

I never knew whether to feel sorry for her or hate her. It was usually an odd mixture of both. She was a miserable creature, that was the only reason why she led such a miserable existence. But to put me and her other children in the path of her self-destruction? I couldn't bring myself to feel any sympathy for how her fuck-ups robbed us of a normal, happy life.

So morbidly obese, she could barely walk without the use of a cane, she leaned heavily on the wall as she stared at us through glassy eyes. The skin on her face was patchy and red, her wild, unkempt hair streaked with gray stuck out in every direction. The stains on her clothes and smells coming from her indicated she had drank and passed out in those clothes for several straight days.

"Melody?" she peered at me like a mole seeing sunlight for the first time.

"We were just leaving, Ma." Every syllable shook as I fought to get the words out. I could feel myself reverting back to a terrified little girl, just trying to stay out of this woman's way. A girl who would say and do anything in the hopes of one peaceful night.

"Nah uh! You ain't leaving until you explain yourself, you ungrateful little bitch! Where the hell have you been?"

Hunter's hand tightened around my arm, a low warning growl already rumbling in his chest. I touched his other hand in an attempt to calm him.

"I don't need to explain anything to you," I replied,

struggling to keep my voice steady. "I became an adult at eighteen and I moved out. Simple as that."

"Bull-SHIT! I didn't give your ass permission to move out! You wanna be an adult? You keep this place running like you used to! I went without a drink for two days because none of these dumbshits knew where to cash my disability checks!"

"Looks like you survived." I couldn't help but sneer. "Unfortunately."

"You are *my* daughter, you ungrateful little tramp! I gave you life and you should be thanking me! I gave birth to all you ungrateful shits, and you left me to suffer! You're supposed to take care of your parents!"

"And you're supposed to protect your kids!" I yelled back, the dam now bursting. Not even Hunter's presence could keep me from holding back. "But you pop them out and endanger them every single day! Do you even know how many swings I took to protect Jeanie, or Bella, or Joey? Do you even remember?"

"Oh, stop being so fuckin' dramatic. Everyone in my family was a bunch of rowdy boozehounds and we turned out fine!"

"Have you looked at yourself?" I cried out, biting back the bile of disgust. "You're *not* fine! None of us are as long as we're with you! That's why I left! Because you pushed us out, but you're no goddamn mother!"

She came at me, screaming obscenities I couldn't even decipher anymore. My throat grew raw like sandpaper, screaming back as Hunter pulled me through the door and slammed it closed behind us. He half carried, half dragged me through the park back to the street, while I could only shake, scream, and claw at my own skin to let out my rage.

5

HUNTER

My heart broke for Mel the moment we pulled up to that dilapidated trailer park. By the time her so-called mother hurled those insults at her, it had shattered into pieces.

She was inconsolable when I brought her back to the RV. Connor and Raz, who'd been leaning against the vehicle casually, suddenly snapped up to attention.

"What happened?" they demanded, muscles tensed and fists clenched as I wrapped Mel in a bear hug and carried her inside. They followed me, itching for a fight as I laid her down on the bed, where she screamed into a pillow and punched the mattress.

"Outside," I directed the two of them. "You too, guys. Move it," I said to Roo and Rinna, who looked at Mel with wide-eyed concern. Everyone reluctantly obeyed me and I followed them out, closing the door behind me to give Mel some privacy.

"Is miss Mel okay?" Roo asked.

"She will be," I assured him. "You guys go sit in Mr. Razvan's truck. The adults are going to talk."

"What the fuck, Hunter?" Raz demanded when the pups were out of earshot, looking around like he was looking for something to punch, too.

"Her mother was there." I shook my head. Just saying the word *mother* felt like the entirely wrong word to use. "They got into an argument."

"An argument? Why do I feel like you're downplaying what really happened?" Connor demanded. "Mel and I have gotten into arguments. She's never turned into a violent, screaming mess."

"That fucking woman," I growled, my own fists clenching at my sides. "Just came out and started calling her names. Insulting her and saying so much shit just because she was there. It was fucking insane, I couldn't believe it."

"Wow, two fucks in two sentences, Hunter. Must've been really bad." Leave it to Connor to tease me in a situation like this.

"It was," I insisted. "And God, she was so fucked up. She had to be the grossest human I've ever seen, looked like shit, smelled like shit. I can't even believe our Mel came out of *that*."

"And you just let her talk to our girl like that?" Raz turned on me, stepping in close to my personal space.

I stared him down. He wouldn't intimidate me. We weren't in his territory anymore, and he wasn't the alpha here. Still, I couldn't ignore the heat in my belly or the surging of blood to my cock when he stepped in close enough to let me inhale his smoky, intoxicating scent.

"I got her out of there, but she didn't even want to

leave at first," I said, regarding him coolly. "Our girl held her own and told that piece of shit excuse for a mother exactly what was on her mind."

"I knew it," Connor chuckled, spinning his wheelchair in a circle. "That girl's got some serious bite and not just in the bedroom."

"But this can't be good." Raz lifted his arm in the direction of the RV, where we could still hear Mel's muffled screams and thumps as she hit things. "Listen to that. She's in so much pain."

"I think the confrontation caused her to let out a lot of anger that she can't put back," I said, scratching at the pale beard on my chin. "She had to put aside what she felt and put on a brave face just to come here. Now, all that's unleashed."

"Sounds like something my old therapist would say, so I think Hunter's right," Connor chimed in. "She just needs to let it out and she'll be okay."

"Fuck, I want to burn that place down to ash," Raz turned and glared at the trailer we just came out of, down at the end of the park. "It's caused her so much misery. So much pain."

"I wouldn't recommend that," I said. "Her siblings still live there. We talked to one of them before the mother came out." I gave them a quick summary of what we talked about with Jeanie, and by then, the screams had dissipated from inside the trailer.

"Let Hunter check on her." Connor reached out and put his hand on Raz's arm when we both turned to go inside. "She doesn't need you making a list of things to burn. He saw firsthand what happened."

With a reluctant nod, Raz leaned his back against the trailer and crossed his arms while I went inside.

Mel laid perfectly still on the bed except for the rise and fall of her erratic breathing. I approached her slowly, as I would an orphaned pup left behind by his pack, and sat down next to her.

"Don't ask me if I'm okay," she said, her voice low and raspy. "Don't try to talk to me about it, please."

"Okay," I responded, and maneuvered behind her. I laid on my side with my chest to her back and draped an arm over her waist. Placing a small kiss on her shoulder, I still kept a few inches of space between us in case she didn't want to be smothered.

After a few moments of tense stiffness between us, she scooted her hips back until the entire length of her body pressed against mine. She sighed and snuggled into me as I wrapped both arms around her, just dropping kisses to her face, neck, and shoulders as I held her.

I wished with all my heart that I could do more for her. But I would only give what she wanted, what she *needed*, and no less. If that was just someone to hold her while she cried, so be it.

Eventually, Connor and the pups climbed aboard, saying nothing and keeping their distance. But everyone wore the same expression of concern.

My ears picked up the sound of Raz's truck engine starting behind us. Connor folded up his wheelchair and lifted himself into the passenger seat, where he patiently waited.

I placed a small kiss on Mel's ear before asking, "Ready to go, little fox?"

She nodded and squeezed my arms a little tighter. "Thank you, Hunter."

I kissed her once more before gently unwrapping myself around her. Connor buckled up in the passenger seat and I took my place behind the wheel. With the turn of a key and no words spoken, we left that hellhole just like Mel did the first time.

With no regrets and no looking back.

6

MELODY

The further Hunter drove us away, the better I felt.

No one ever left me alone, whether Roo and Rinna kept close watch over me or Connor lifted himself up and took a nap beside me. Their presence reminded me of where I was now and what I really escaped from.

The sun faded low as we neared the Alabama-Georgia border. I sat up in bed, feeling like the dead rising as I stretched. Hunter caught my eye in the rearview mirror as he turned off the freeway.

"You okay, little fox?" he asked, lifting his chin slightly as I came up behind him and smoothed my hands down his chest.

"I am now," I answered, placing my chin on top of his head. "But I don't think Jeanie is, and that's what kills me."

He took one hand off the steering wheel and brought one of my hands to his lips. "If she's anything like you, she'll make it through. She's tough, and now she has a lifeline."

In the passenger seat, Connor spun his phone on the dashboard. "How many times did you call CPS while living there, babe?"

"Hundreds," I told him. "But they're so backed up with more urgent cases. I stopped calling when I was around sixteen because Mom threatened us. Getting split up would mean fewer dependents for her, which meant less money. I'm sure she's brainwashed the younger ones into not calling, too."

"They'll get out," Hunter insisted with a small undertone of a growl. "We'll help you get them all out. Even if we have to adopt them ourselves."

"That's even more complicated," I sighed, running my fingers through his pale, silky hair. "But you guys are amazing for even offering."

We meandered through the small nameless town, looking for a place to park our two large vehicles that would attract the least amount of attention. A Motel 6 passing on our left side reminded me of my earlier desire that day.

"Hey! Do you guys want to go for a swim later?"

"I dunno if you noticed, babe," Connor laughed. "But I'm kind of missing my flippers."

"Con, your arms are strong enough to pull your entire body weight." I rolled my eyes at him. "I'm dying to just take a dip and wash this whole day away."

"That sounds good to me," Hunter agreed, circling back toward the motel, which probably thoroughly confused Razvan following us. "I'm not sure how the fire breather will feel about it."

"It's not like he'll melt," I squeezed his shoulder. "The

guy pulls around a bathtub, he can't be that scared of going underwater."

"Did y'all bring your bathing suits or am I missing something here?" Connor inquired.

I climbed into his lap, facing him with a wicked smile. "Who needs bathing suits when we have birthday suits?"

"Sweet Jesus," he groaned, his large hands pawing at my waist as his pupils dilated. "I'm in, as long as there's a shallow end."

"One little naked run through the woods and she's an exhibitionist already," Hunter laughed.

"What the fuck did I miss while holed up in that hospital?" Connor demanded.

Hunter and I recounted how our first threesome began —vaguely at first, but Connor thirstily demanded more details. While we filled him in, Hunter parked the massive vehicle on a side street just behind the motel. We could get into the pool after just a short walk and a hop over the fence.

"Why didn't y'all just fuck right there in the bathtub?" Connor asked as Hunter removed the keys from the ignition.

"It was too small," I told him in a fit of giggles, my stomach flipping at discussing it so casually like this. "All three of us wouldn't have fit."

"Y'all just need to get more creative," he said with a mocking shake of his head. "I'll show you how it's done," he added huskily.

"Oy!" Razvan hollered from outside the trailer with three quick knocks to the door. "Why are we stopping here, wolf-boy?"

Roo opened the door to let him in and Hunter nodded

at him from the driver's seat. "Mel wants to go for a swim. You down?"

"A naked swim," Connor added.

"How can I refuse when you put it that way?" Raz crossed his arms and sent a look my way that had me squirming in Connor's lap. Something told me that no amount of water would be putting out this fire.

"We should wait 'til it's dark, so we can sneak in easier," Connor drummed his fingertips on my hips. "Maybe grab some food first. I saw a grocery store nearby."

"Can we swim too?" Roo piped up.

"Nope." Hunter turned in his seat to face his son's pout. "It's an adults-only swim. I need you guys to stay here and guard the vehicles. It's a very important job and I'm counting on you, okay?"

"Why do we always get left out of the adult stuff?" Roo whined, stamping his feet.

"One day you'll understand, little man," Razvan ruffled his hair.

The affectionate contact surprised me. Raz hadn't had much interaction with the pups, but right then he looked down at Hunter's mini-me with an endearing expression. Hunter noticed it too, but his expression seemed more conflicted.

Regardless, Razvan's placating seemed to work as Roo stopped complaining, although he remained pouty. We all assured him how important it was to guard the vehicles before the four of us set out in search of food.

As we walked through the streets of the small, southern town and then its even smaller supermarket, I couldn't tell which one of us got the most stares. Or maybe it was our group as a whole?

Hunter turned heads with his imposing height, chiseled features and ethereal beauty. Men and women alike stopped in their tracks to stare at him. Razvan's rough-and-tumble, tattooed form put the fear of God on the faces of old ladies, brought on lustful looks from younger women, and incited jealous glares from men. Connor, running circles around us all in his wheelchair, brought on looks of curiosity, then admiration and respect when they noticed the dog tags around his neck and the strength in his massive arms.

And then there was me, the leggy, doe-eyed, raven-haired girl in the middle of this band of misfits, pushing the buggy around while yelling at my goofball men to behave. Could this be our version of reality one day? The four of us, shopping for groceries on a normal weekday evening.

The thought stayed with me as we checked out and carried our bags back to the trailer. We ate from our microwave meals while standing or sitting around Connor's tiny kitchen space. Was it a pipe dream to picture all of us having dinner together in an actual kitchen? At a table big enough for all of us to sit around, even the pups? Could we even have a bedroom one day with a bed big enough to fit all four of us?

It felt like a fantasy, but in that moment, I realized I wanted it more than anything. A normal life with my perfectly imperfect family. The family I'd chosen.

Night fell as we finished eating and put away the rest of the supplies. A giddy excitement came over me as we walked down the street, talking in hushed whispers. I felt like I was in high school again, sneaking into a house party.

The motel pool glittered like a lagoon at an oasis from the other side of the wrought-iron fence. Most of the nearby rooms were dark. Hopefully, that meant they were vacant. Not a soul was in sight. The deck chairs were still laid out and even some folded towels were piled on a table. It was our own private paradise.

"Up you go, *steluța*." Razvan lifted me by the waist so I could climb over the fence with all the grace of an elephant. He and Hunter followed me over with animal-like agility.

"Shit, wait." Hunter landed lightly on his feet, then immediately turned to look at Connor on the other side. "I'll come back over, Con."

"Boys, please," Connor scoffed, holding up a hand. "Remember who the fuck you're talking to."

We all watched dumbfounded as Connor lifted himself from his wheelchair and swung himself over the fence with even more grace and agility than the two shifters—never once using his legs.

"Alright then, show-off," Razvan laughed, peeling off his shirt. "Race ya to the pool!"

"Now I'd be foolish to accept that." Connor seated himself on the concrete pool deck as he began removing his own clothes. "Don't judge a fish on its ability to climb a tree or however the saying goes."

"Fair enough." Raz's eyes danced mischievously over to Hunter. "Wolf?"

The two of them froze in a tense moment of time, like a pair of duelists watching each other in the beginning of a standoff. In the next moment, they hurriedly undressed. My eyes doubled in size as they unzipped their jeans and hilariously hopped around as they fought to get out of their pant legs. I couldn't breathe from laughing so hard as they finally stripped down to their underwear and were neck and neck as they raced to the pool's edge.

Hunter won the race by a few inches, his height and long arms giving him the advantage as he cut through the water like a dolphin.

"Well, *that* wasn't sexual at all," Connor muttered as he pressed up and walked on his hands next to me to the edge of the pool.

7

MELODY

I looked at Connor in surprise. "You, uh, know about that?"

"If Hunter didn't tell you, I was going to do the honors." He winked up at me as he swiped a towel from a nearby deck chair.

"Get in, you two! It feels great," Razvan called. He and Hunter both surfaced and swam back across to greet us.

I lowered myself to sit on the edge and dipped one foot in the water.

"Ohh, it really does," I sighed.

"I'm headin' for the shallows," Connor muttered as he kept hand-walking to the opposite end, where the pool bottom gently sloped upward to meet the edge.

"You can ride on my back, buddy," Razvan cackled. "I won't let you drown."

"Hell no! I ain't nobody's jetpack!"

"Coming in, little fox?"

Hunter swam up next to my dangling feet, his hair

spreading out around him like a halo on the surface of the water.

"Are you kidding?" I pulled my top over my head, stripping down to my bra. "This was *my* fantastic idea."

Raz swam up next to him and grabbed my ankle, an evil grin on his face as he looked up at me. "You need to do your fantastic idea faster."

"Don't you dare, Raz!" I kicked my legs in warning, splashing water in both of their faces. "I can't get these clothes wet. We need to find a laundromat tomorrow."

"Whatever. Hurry up and get in."

They watched like a pair of hungry sharks as I removed my feet from the water and slid my shorts off my legs. After a moment's hesitation, I made off with my bra and panties, too. Yeah, maybe I talked about birthday suits earlier, but being nude in public still made me a little nervous.

"Ahhh." The coolness of the water shocked me as I slid in. I held my breath as my entire face dipped below the surface, my toes touching the bottom a moment later.

"See?" Razvan wrapped an arm around my waist as I resurfaced. "Feels amazing."

Before I could reply, he lifted my whole torso just above the surface and threw me.

"Mel in the middle!" Hunter laughed, kissing me through my scream as he caught me, then threw me back to Razvan.

"Ha!" Supported by the buoyancy of the water, I wrapped my legs around Raz's waist, smiling triumphantly. "Can't get rid of me now."

"Like I would ever want to," he murmured before

kissing me deeply, his lips cool from the water while the inside of his mouth still burned hot.

Before I could lose myself too much in kissing him, a pair of arms wrapped around my middle and dragged my upper body away from him through the water. I dipped my head back to see Hunter with a playful pout on his face.

"No fair," he grumbled before kissing me deeply. "The winner should get the girl."

"You barely won." Raz rolled his eyes. "All because of your damn height."

"You already had a head start with your shirt off! I beat you fair and square."

I found their bickering adorable. With my legs still wrapped around Raz, I alternated between kissing him and Hunter as they both drifted closer within sandwiching distance. While they shut up for the moments my lips were on theirs, they seemed more interested in trash talking than any kind of sandwiched fun.

"Screw you guys, I'm hanging out with Connor."

Raz barely seemed to notice when my legs unwrapped from him. He and Hunter were now in some heated debate about the fastest land animals.

Connor sat against the pool wall nearby, the water up to his shoulders.

"Hey, are you actually floating?" I asked as I doggy-paddled over to him.

"Nah, there's a ledge to sit on," he smirked. "Come here, babe."

I drifted over until he pulled me into his lap, the fabric of his boxer shorts teasing me through the water.

"I like watching you with them," he murmured, his

mouth on my ear. "They're just what I wanted for you—good guys you can lean on when you've had enough of me."

"You know I hate it when you talk about yourself like that." I turned to face him. "So please don't. Not while I'm just trying to relax in a pool with you guys. And anyway," I wrapped an arm around his shoulders, creating droplets of water in the crevices of his muscles. "After we get to Georgia, I hope they help you see what you're worth."

"I know I'm worth more just having you with me." He kissed me long and deeply. "But I'm still skeptical of this place. I still don't know why this guy's so interested in me."

The non-profit center we were going to was headed by a colleague of Dr. Harman, the doctor who treated Connor for his concussion after his fall. His center specialized in providing services to combat veterans, including new prosthetics for Connor's legs free of charge.

"How's your pain been?" I asked him, massaging around his knees.

"Better," he admitted with a soft groan of pleasure from the touch. "Easily tolerable lately. I think he was right about pressure on the nerves."

"See? You should listen to doctors," I teased, kissing him on the cheek. "And to me."

"I'm working on it, babe." He lifted his forest-green eyes to me, bright, clear and full of adoration that made my heart skip. "I'm not used to people caring so much. Accepting help feels... weak."

"It's not," I insisted. "And you have three of us willing to help you, with no questions asked."

"I know." His arms tightened around my waist. "Believe me, I know."

His skin was cool, but quickly heated as he held my

body flush to his. The mix of hot and cold sensations sent my nerves into overdrive as his firm grip palmed my ass, his tongue invaded my mouth, and he pulled me toward his growing erection.

Goosebumps erected on my skin and not because of the temperature. We were going to do this here? Now? It wasn't quite public, but close enough. The thought scared and thrilled me as Connor's rough hands enveloped my breasts in warmth before releasing them to the cold water again.

A sudden, loud splash broke our kiss and made me look over my shoulder. Hunter and Raz were roughhousing, wrestling and grabbing each other to dunk underwater. They laughed and moved aggressively, still in a competitive spirit and not wanting to let the other win. But I also saw the ways their eyes heated, and the way their fingers trailed against the other to prolong their touch.

"God, look at you, babe," Connor growled, his voice thick with desire. "You're so fucking turned on right now."

"I—" My excuse cut off with a gasp as his hand cupped between my thighs, and only then did I feel the true liquid heat building like a volcano within me, without the coolness of the water to temper it.

"Turn around," Connor instructed. "Keep watching them. They get you so hot, don't they?"

"Yes," I admitted, spinning in his lap to press my back to his chest. He cupped one hand around my breasts and sent the other down to caress my clit.

"Do you want to see them touch each other like I'm touching you?" His voice rumbled against my back and my neck, where his hot mouth nipped at my cool skin. "Do you want to see both of their cocks out, pleasing each other?"

"Yes," I gasped, arching against him. Like he had been there, he voiced every dirty fantasy in my head ever since Hunter, Raz, and I spent the night together. And as I watched them, wrestling and play-fighting for dominance, I could see it come to life before my very eyes.

Raz pounced on Hunter's back, wrapping his arms around his neck in a choke-hold and his tattooed legs around the wolf shifter's slender, pale waist. Hunter's response was to fall backward, creating a huge splash and sending both of them underwater. When they surfaced separately, Hunter swam over and captured Raz in his own headlock, their faces close enough to kiss.

Nothing about the sexual tension between them made them any less masculine. If anything, their displays of strength and playful violence made them even more masculine, and got me even hotter.

"What if I fucked you while they fucked at the same time?" Connor went on, talking low enough in my ear so only I could hear. "They'd get so hot watching you and you'd come so sweetly on my cock watching them."

"Connor..." I thrashed madly against him, the vision playing out in my head like an extension of the one happening before me. God, just the mental picture he described was as hot as his fingers stroking me, his rough kisses on my neck and shoulders.

If Raz and Hunter had any idea of what we were doing or imagining, they gave no indication of it. The two alpha shifters also showed no signs of stopping. They'd keep this up until sunrise if they could. Based on strength alone, they seemed perfectly evenly matched.

Raz's dark inked designs were a beautiful contrast against Hunter's pale, unmarked skin. For the past several minutes, they moved too fast for me to really enjoy the visual, but right then, they started to slow.

Raz clung to Hunter's back again, his arms around his neck, but instead of a chokehold, he held on loosely, his tattooed hands skimming over the top of Hunter's chest. For the briefest moment, Hunter touched his hands as if to hold them, but quickly changed his mind and let them drop to his sides with a small splash.

The dragon shifter's hands drifted over him like in a caress, but could have also been interpreted as a simple change in grip. What could not have been mistaken was how Hunter's face turned toward his. Raz's forehead touched his temple in a small but indisputable gesture of affection.

Their eyes met. All splashing and horseplay ceased for this moment of stillness, of tranquility. Hunter slowly turned to face Raz, their gazes locked on each other and standing close, so close...

"Ah-mmph!"

Connor clamped a hand over my mouth as his skilled fingers sent my thrashing overboard into an orgasm. I was so entranced by watching the shifters, the wave of pleasure snuck up on me unnoticed and took over my body like a demonic possession. Connor's words, his hands on me, and the unbearably hot images dancing in my head combined into such a perfect storm, Raz and Hunter only had to look at each other like *that* to send me over the edge.

But now, they looked at me with expressions I couldn't read. The corners of Raz's mouth tipped up in a knowing smirk, but flickers of shame and embarrassment flashed through his eyes. Hunter cast his gaze down to the surface of the water, but I thought I could see a smile playing on his lips too.

"Shit." Connor shoved me off his lap before any of us could say a word. "Somebody's coming."

"Mel already did," Raz laughed softly.

"No, lizard-brain, I feel footsteps on the concrete. We're about to get caught!"

The four of us sprung into frantic, hurried action. I climbed out and wrapped a towel around myself, praying it would stay on until we cleared the fence. Walking on his hands, Connor was the first to reach the fence, pulling himself up and vaulting over like a gymnast.

Raz and Hunter quickly swam to the end of the pool and pulled themselves up, racing to the fence.

"Hey! Stop!" someone yelled over running footsteps on the concrete.

"Come on, Mel!" Hunter waited for me as Raz scrambled over the top.

Still dripping wet and only in his boxer briefs, he grabbed my waist and hoisted me up. Raz held his arms out to catch me on the other side as I struggled to keep my towel on and also not fall like a sack of potatoes.

"Let's go!"

Hunter landed soundlessly on his feet and immediately took off running toward the RV. Connor was already in his wheelchair, speeding down the sidewalk ahead of us. Raz ran with me, my hand in his while the other clutched my towel to my chest.

One by one, we slapped the side of the RV like we were kids playing tag and it was our home base. Breathless and exhilarated, we all looked at each other between wide, wicked smiles and hushed, maniacal laughter. Maybe it was juvenile, but fuck, that was fun and risky.

"Shit!" I exclaimed, looking down at myself and then at the three guys, still dripping wet and only in their underwear, which left little to the imagination. "We left our clothes behind!"

No one said a word. After a moment of exchanging awkward glances at each other, we all burst into peals of laughter once again.

8

MELODY

After drying off and curling up snugly between Raz and Connor in the bed of the RV, I tried reaching out to the mysterious predator shifter once again. Since feeling his despair and watching him kill as if I were doing it myself, I felt uneasy about trying again. What would happen if I tried to communicate with a dead shifter? Did I want to know?

Regardless, I had to try. His presence felt stronger, and so much closer last time. Unfortunately, that meant I could feel the damage done to him in even crisper detail. He had been starved, weakened, and drugged. I got the sense that he'd been in his animal shift for so long, those predatory, survival instincts grew dominant inside him and made his human side weaker.

If his captors didn't know he shifted, I hoped that was a good thing. It meant he wouldn't be displayed as a partially shifted freak like Raz or Hunter had been. But if they figured he was just an animal, they could be treating him even worse.

I closed my eyes and took deep, steadying breaths. Trying to communicate directly with my mind was like yelling down a hallway. If I successfully reached who I was talking to, I could feel them somewhere in the same way, their presence amplified as if through a tunnel. Last time, the shifter felt as though he was at the other end of the hallway.

But now? I nearly gasped at his closeness. It felt like he was right next to me.

I sensed a human man nearly as tall as Hunter, with caramel skin and glossy black hair. His large eyes danced with an array of colors that took my breath away—bluish green with gold flecks, like some kind of precious stone. Dark stubble coated his angular lower jaw. He came through clearly, a shift in his energy told me he knew I was there but something was wrong.

I thought you'd abandoned me. His voice was filled with relief and longing.

I'm sorry, I answered. *It's been a rough, busy journey. But I'm so close to you now.*

It might be too late, he answered, full of sorrow.

Why? I demanded. *Why can I only sense the human side of you, not your animal shift?*

My tiger is heavily sedated. He's barely alive, he replied. *They will most likely dispose of him tomorrow. And... that will be the end of me too.*

No! I cried. *I won't let them! We're so close.*

Don't worry about me, young shaman, he said gently. *I'll die knowing there's still one of you out there. It gives me peace knowing a human who understands us. Help the poor shifter who takes my place. After these long, painful years, I'm ready to let go.*

Please, don't. Hot tears spilled down my face. Don't give up yet. I just found you. At least tell me your name.

It's Arjun, he replied. *My shift is a Bengal tiger. I'm probably the last. My family is all gone, but in case you find another one of us, tell them what I did. I want them to know.*

The man you killed? I asked.

Yes. His mental voice took on a viciousness that sent a shiver of fear through me. *I spilled the blood of my captor and it was delicious. I'll never regret it, not even if it sends my soul to Naraka. He's in whatever hell he belongs, and I want my brethren to know I sent him there.*

I'll tell them, I promised. *And I'll make sure every one of those humans who laid a finger on you gets what's coming to them. But I'll need your help, Arjun. So I need you to live.*

No response came.

"Steluța?"

"Hm?" Hovering in the state between awake and sleep, my legs kicked out as Razvan pulled me toward the world of the living.

"You were mumbling in your sleep." Soft lips and a split tongue caressed the skin of my neck in the dark.

"I talked to him," I whimpered, the conversation flooding back. "As soon as everyone's awake, we have to move. They're going to kill him."

"Shh, calm down," my dragon soothed me. "Tell me what happened."

When I relayed the conversation and said he was a

tiger, Razvan's grip tightened on me so hard it was nearly painful.

"A Bengal tiger?" he repeated, his tone incredulous. "You're sure? Did you get his name?"

"Arjun," I said. "Why?"

His fingers slowly loosened around my arm. I felt his short, buzzed hair tickle my skin as he rested his head on my shoulder. He was shaking slightly, as if holding back laughter.

"Razvan?" I felt for his face in the dark. The skin near his eye was slightly raised from his tattoo there. "What is it?"

"That striped bastard," he chuckled. "I should have known he would've had a connection to you, too. Even though it's been years since we've talked."

I couldn't believe my luck. "You know him?"

"We were forced to perform together," he answered quietly. "I set things on fire, he jumped over and through them. Poor cat was terrified of fire and had burns all over himself. I taught him to do it as safely as possible and we formed an unlikely friendship. When Nigel came and rescued a bunch of us, I went with him. Arjun went his own way. It fucking kills me that he got recaptured, although I could see his view of things. He didn't trust humans at all."

"Jesus, what are the odds?" I breathed. "That I found Hunter, you, and him all within such a short time. It makes me wonder how many shifters really walk among humans."

"It must be the shaman in you." He gave my waist an affectionate squeeze. "We just can't stop ourselves from gravitating toward you. But you're so naturally irresistible, you just happened to catch Connor first."

"Stop," I smacked his chest playfully.

"It's true," he laughed, pulling me in closer to tickle my ribs. "And don't worry, *steluța*. We won't let anything happen to Arjun. I already have an idea."

"Oh, yeah?" I nuzzled under his chin. "Let's hear it."

"Well, seems this carnival needs a new ringmaster for one." I heard the smile in his voice. "Or ringmistress, rather."

"Raz!" I gasped, thumping his chest again, victoriously this time. "You're a genius."

"Not quite, but I have my moments," he chuckled. "And I'll audition for a knife thrower or pyro, whatever they need. We'll find our way in and get him out."

"Sounds like a plan." My fingers traced the contours of his collarbone in the darkness, then drifted down over his sternum.

"What is it?" he asked, as if he could sense a question on my mind through the way I touched him.

My fingertips paused just over his abs. "Were you and Arjun ever... more than friends?"

His breath hitched, and I felt his pulse quicken, but his voice remained calm.

"No, we weren't." His hand wrapped around mine. "We bonded over being two shifters thrown into a horrible situation. We had each other's backs, but it never went beyond that." He paused for a breath. "Why do you ask me that?"

I swallowed, my throat going dry. "I don't want to make anyone uncomfortable. But in the pool, you seemed to have chemistry with..."

"With Hunter," he finished for me in a low voice.

We both paused to listen to the slow, deep breathing of Hunter and the pups. They were curled up a few feet away on the floor in wolf form. Hunter said he found it easier to sleep that way with not enough beds to go around.

"If you wanted to pursue something with him," I whispered. "I wouldn't mind at all."

"Did he say anything to you?" he whispered back with a mixture of eagerness and uncertainty.

"I... promised not to say anything," I answered sheepishly.

"And yet you have said so much already," he chuckled, pressing his lips to my forehead. "I'll think this over," he added. "And thank you, *steluţa*."

"For what?"

"For not making a big deal of it," he answered. "For, you know, accepting us."

"He grows fur and a tail. You grow wings and scales," I giggled. "Being attracted to men isn't even half of what makes you a freak."

"Oh?" He said the word like a challenge, his arm sliding around my backside to grab a plentiful handful of my ass. "What else makes me a freak?"

"The fact that you like me," I giggled, squirming in his grip.

"I got two other men here who would disagree," he groaned huskily into my neck. "Once we get Arjun out, maybe even a third."

"No way," I sighed. "The three of you give me enough to deal with already."

"Oh, but you have so much fun with us," he teased.

"And what if the wolf and I hook up and you're still craving a sandwich?"

"Thinking about that already, are you?" I teased him back, but my core flooded with heat at the thought. Connor touching me while Raz and Hunter wrestled in the pool was already too hot for words, but a threesome while watching the two of them? I couldn't imagine anything more utterly, delightfully sinful.

But the thought of Arjun was a sobering one. I hadn't even met the guy, despite talking to him and sensing his mental state. Fitting him into a threesome was beyond getting ahead of myself.

"One thing at a time, I suppose," Raz sighed, smoothing his hands along my back side. "Let's give the others a few more hours to sleep. Then we'll let a tiger loose."

9

MELODY

"Why does this story sound awfully familiar?" Connor narrowed his eyes at me. "Rescuing another mistreated animal in need? What are we, the SPCA on wheels?"

"Come on, you had so much fun last time," Hunter slapped him on the back, nearly making him spill his coffee. "It all worked out, right?"

"Barely," Connor grumbled, rubbing a hand over his eyes in an attempt to wake up. "You're lucky you came with cute kids and the natural ability to bring home bacon."

"Relax, babe." I slithered between Raz and Hunter to stand between Connor's thighs. "You won't be part of this one. It'll just be me and Raz."

"Like *hell* I won't be part of it." He set down his coffee and gripped the edges of the counter as if he would jump off. "Just from what you told me, this place sounds ten times shadier than Drowningville. You need more backup going in there."

"Remember what I told you." I returned his narrowed-eyed threatening gaze. "You need to care for yourself. Hunter will drive you on to the nonprofit center. I need you fit and mobile."

"I am!" he protested. "Didn't you see me swinging over that fence last night? I can keep up with any of you."

"I know, babe." My voice stayed calm as I circled my fingers around his knees. "But if it's really worse than Drowningville, it could have a lot of potential triggers for you. I need you in top shape mentally too."

"Jesus tap dancing Christ, Mel. I'm not some goddamn snowflake."

"This isn't negotiable." I folded my arms across my chest, holding his eye contact as I dared him to fight me. "Raz and I have this handled. You're going to where you need to go. That's the end of it."

His jaw clenched. His knuckles whitened as he gripped the edges of the counter even harder. A long, tense silence passed between us that wasn't sexual for once. I didn't move, and neither did he. Finally, he let out a long breath as he dropped his gaze.

"Fine."

Satisfied, I gave him a curt nod and grabbed my own coffee cup to fill from the pot.

"I'm so fucking horny right now," Raz muttered. A slug on the arm from Connor wiped the smirk off his face.

THE SUN just began to rise as we set out on the road. We shut off the GPS and just followed where my instincts told me to go.

"Northeast," I told Hunter. "Just start heading in that direction."

The small town faded away and turned to long, country road. We drove for hours, only stopping for gas once as the day dragged on and the miles flew past us. Not once did any of the guys question or second-guess me. They just followed where I said to go.

Arjun's presence grew stronger with each passing mile. I rubbed my fingers together, the pads feeling thick and calloused from the multiple burns he sustained. The beginnings of a roar rumbled from deep in my chest. His tiger wasn't done. He still wanted to fight and take as many of those wretched humans down with him as possible.

That will to live gave me hope as we rolled through some of the most beat-down settlements I'd ever seen. The word *town* couldn't accurately describe the decrepit shacks and trailers plopped down on either side of the road, surrounded by rusted trucks, tall, dry grass, and tarps cluttered with various debris. It was like someone took my old trailer park and decided to display our redneck poverty as a roadside attraction.

"What a dump. Can people actually live in places like this?" Connor muttered, staring out the window. "Makes Mel's old place look like a resort."

The dirt road eventually turned to gravel and then cracked pavement riddled with potholes as the structures slowly came closer together into what actually resembled a small town. A rusted sign marked with bullet holes read, "Welcome to Fulmer" as it passed us on the right-hand side.

"Looks like we found where the tiger is." Hunter

nodded up ahead at the horizon, where a rusted, rickety Ferris wheel loomed over the town like a giant, bloodshot eye.

"That thing is *not* up to any modern safety standards," Connor added. "Looks like it'll fall over if you sneeze on it."

"Imagine how the rest of the carnival is," I muttered, dread filling the pit of my stomach.

We pulled over to a side street, Razvan bringing his truck right up behind us. Connor pulled out his phone and checked his GPS while the dragon joined us in the RV.

"I'll be damned," Connor declared. "The nonprofit center is only a half-hour drive from here, in a neighboring town that's much nicer than this."

"So we'll be close." Hunter crossed his arms. "That's good."

"Not close enough," Connor murmured as he pulled me into his lap in the passenger seat. "Babe, I'll never forgive myself if anything happened to you."

"Nothing will harm her, Con," Raz said with such firm conviction, it made my thighs press together. "You have my word."

"I really hope your word means something, dragon-man." Connor turned his sharp gaze to him. "Because if she even breaks a nail, I will choke out the fire from your lungs myself."

"I'd expect nothing less," Raz answered solemnly.

"You just focus on healing your pain." I wrapped an arm around Connor's neck. "Take care of this mind and body I love so much."

"Are you kidding? I won't be able to stop worrying about you for one goddamn second." He crushed me to his chest, pressing a kiss to my mouth that sent flutters all the way down to my toes.

Eventually, he released me to Hunter, who kissed me with playful nips of his teeth that left me clinging to him and gasping for more. Damn these men who knew how to make me miss them.

"Call me with an update as soon as you have one," Conner said.

"I will," I promised, lowering my mouth to his for a final long, lingering kiss. "Hopefully we'll see you before the day is over."

After hugging the pups and promising I'd be back, Raz and I exited the RV and headed toward his truck.

"Have you ever auditioned for a carnival job before?" I asked as I slid in next to him and buckled my seatbelt.

"Nope," he answered. "Before Nigel found me, everything was involuntary. After, he always had a job for me. I didn't even need to ask." His eyes slid over, drinking in the length of my legs before he placed a hand on my thigh. "How did your first audition go?"

"All I had to do was wear this," I laughed, gesturing to my shorts and tank top, "on a hot summer day. They put me wherever they needed people until Connor found me."

"Seems like we won't have much trouble at all," he grinned as we pulled away from the curb. We waved to Hunter and Connor, who turned and began driving in the opposite direction.

"Why did you stay working for Nigel?" I asked the burning question on my mind for weeks as we approached the ominous Ferris wheel. "After being forced to perform, why would you do it voluntarily?"

"What else could I do?" he replied, eyes flickering

across the road. "I barely spoke English. I had no true skills besides what I was taught for the stage. I chose to cover myself in ink, which makes some people assume I'm a criminal. Plus," his voice softened, "I did leave for a bit, to return to Romania. Only to find I was no more welcome there as when they sent me away."

We pulled up to a red light, and he turned to me, cupped my chin, and pressed a soft kiss to my lips with a light caress of his tongue.

"My tongue was the last thing I did while I was there." He stuck his tongue out and flicked both sides independently. "A way to remember my homeland and my dual nature without having to see it all the time like a tattoo."

"I didn't know you could place meaning on it like that," I said.

He shrugged. "You can attach meaning to anything if you want to. Or not. Many of my tattoos mean nothing. I just wanted a certain look."

I grabbed his hand and returned it to its place on my thigh, where he gave me an affectionate squeeze.

"I'm sorry your home rejected you," I breathed, watching his side profile as he drove. "I hope you feel at home with us... with me."

"*Steluţa*," he mumbled gruffly. "Being with you and the others is the closest thing to home I ever felt. I'll stay with you as long as you'll have me."

We circled around the carnival grounds, looking for a place to park. The entire place was so poorly laid out and disorganized, like the staff had been high on meth when they set up. Which probably wasn't far from the truth.

After parking, we walked around looking for someone to talk about getting hired. Raz took my hand and held me close to his side, clearly taking his promise to Connor seriously. His word meant a great deal, and he sought to prove that to my Marine.

Wandering around the back, we found a cluster of tents and trailers, much like the ones back in Drowningville. However, they weren't roped off or truly separated in any way from the main grounds. While it was the middle of the day and nearly empty, any attendee could just wander back here much like we had.

I rubbed my arms, chills covering me despite the sweltering heat. This place gave me so many similar vibes to Drowningville, if not worse. Maybe because I no longer ignored my instincts, or being aware of my shaman abilities made me more sensitive to them, but I knew deep in my bones this place was the epitome of corruption and exploitation.

Raz knocked on a few trailer doors with no answer. At the fourth one, he barely knocked once before the door slammed open and made us jump a step back.

A dwarf of a man, only about four feet tall and reeking of alcohol, peered up at us.

"Can I help y'all?" he asked in a nasal voice.

"Hi!" I answered cheerfully, plastering on a smile. "We're performers looking for jobs. Do you know who we talk to about that?"

"Me," he grunted. "But there ain't no jobs to go 'round."

I chewed my lip. If their ringmaster had died a day ago, it most likely wasn't public knowledge that the job was open yet. I couldn't act like I knew about the tiger's attack.

"Are you sure?" I pressed, sending my grin wider.

"We're both very multi-talented. I'm positive we can add something to your carnival."

The small man eyed me up and down in a way that made my skin crawl, much like the way Syko had.

"What do ya do?" he inquired.

"I do ah, burlesque," I stammered. "And I was ring-mistress at my last job."

Raz shot me a warning look before answering for himself. "Sword swallowing," he grunted. "And fire breath-ing. Often both at the same time. Anything to do with sharp objects and fire, I'm your man."

The dwarf burped and rubbed his chin. "Well," he began. "We do have one opening, come to think of it. Maybe two. I can see about doin' some quick auditions if y'all want to perform tonight." He eyed me again with a predatory grin. "You first, dollface. If I like what I see, your man can show us what he's got, too."

10

MELODY

"**S**ure!" I squeaked, smiling so hard that my cheeks hurt. "Whatever works. We're ready when you are."

The man grinned back, thoroughly pleased. "I'll gather some folks and get a stage ready. Come back in an hour. Name's Phil, by the way."

"I'm uh, Cherry!" I reached out to accept his sticky handshake.

"Damn ripe and sweet like one," he grunted, holding onto my hand for far longer than was comfortable before turning to Raz. "And you are?"

"Alexei," he answered without missing a beat.

"Where the hell you from?"

"Siberia," Raz answered. "A cold-ass, far north region of Russia."

"Thought you sounded Russian," Phil observed. "Alright, folks. Come back in an hour."

"Why the hell did you say that?" Raz demanded the

moment we walked away from the cluster of trailers. "Burlesque? *Steluţa*, do you know what that means?"

"It's like tasteful stripping, right? Like what Ally and all her friends did."

He glared at the mention of the last girl he slept with before me, the one who nearly drove us apart for good because she couldn't handle him only having casual feelings for her.

"I have a feeling *tasteful* isn't what these people have in mind," he muttered under his breath. "Why didn't you just say ringmistress?"

"I didn't want him to catch on that we knew the last one just died," I answered. "I'm sorry, Raz. I panicked for a second. I didn't want to arouse suspicion."

"No, you're just going to be arousing everything else now."

"Jealous?" I teased, trying to make light of the situation despite my stomach churning at what I would have to do in front of these people.

"I share you with two other men," he growled. "I'm not jealous, I just don't want people looking at you like that. Whistling and yelling degrading things at you... *Steluţa*, I don't think you realize how burlesque shows get. Nigel had hard rules in place for the dancers' safety. At other places, they get really, really rowdy. Honestly, it's a prostitution front for places like this. That guy probably thought I was your pimp."

Shit.

"Shit," I voiced.

"Yeah," he agreed, running a hand over his short, buzzed hair. "We're kind of backed into a corner now. I don't know how we're going to get out of this one."

I looked around at the old worn down booths and rides that had certainly seen better days. Rusted shipping containers laid on the dry grass in the distance. My instincts pulled me there like I was attached to a long, invisible string.

"Why not see if we find a tiger?" I said, nodding my head toward the containers. "If we do, who says we have to stick around?"

"Jesus Christ." Raz ran a hand down his face. "Now I know how Connor must've felt when you rescued the wolves."

But he followed as I started heading in that direction. "Don't act like you're on a rescue mission," he growled in my ear as he caught up. "You want to not arouse suspicion? Walk slower. Meander and look around at the booths. Look at me and laugh. Smile and kiss me."

"You just can't keep your hands off me," I said in a low voice before laughing heartily and giving him a deep, full kiss.

"True," he murmured, his warm breath tickling my lips. "But they do have eyes on us. Do you feel them? With an operation this shady, they're always looking out for under-cover cops trying to bust them."

"Damn it." I leaned my head on his shoulder and stuck my hand in his rear jeans pocket. "So you're saying even if we find him, we're not likely to walk out with him anytime soon?"

"I think chances of that are nearly zero." He slid a tattooed arm around my waist and looked up, craning his neck to stare at the top of the Ferris wheel. "Fuck, the thought of you taking clothes off for these assholes just makes my blood boil."

"Connor would be downright murderous." I was silently glad that it was Raz next to me and not my overprotective Marine.

"And Hunter?" Raz squeezed my hip. "What would he do?"

"He'd rip their throats out in the most calm, detached, serial-killer fashion you'd ever see."

"That's what I thought," he chuckled, his voice softening and eyes growing dreamy at the thought of our wolf shifter.

My fingers tensed in his back pocket, realizing I no longer thought of Hunter as mine, but *ours*. Warmth and comfort filled me at the thought of the two of them snuggling together, much like we were now. Already I couldn't wait for the four of us to reunite so my shifters could have their chance to become closer.

Arms around each other like any ordinary couple on a date, we slowly meandered closer to the shipping containers. I didn't even have to focus to sense Arjun inside one of them. The human side of him still felt quiet and far away, but I could've reached out and felt the dense fur and powerful feline muscles of his tiger as if he was right next to me.

With one mental touch, that power wasn't just next to me, but within me. I was so hungry. I needed to kill. I needed the comfort of a mate.

"Did you just purr?" Raz asked, amusement in his voice.

"*Hrrrrr?*"

My hand flew to my throat in shock. "Holy shit! That came from me?"

"*Steluța.*" He stood squarely in front of me, blocking

anyone from seeing my face. A smile crept across his lips. "What big teeth you have."

Trembling, my hand crept up from my throat to my chin, where two long canines jutted down past my lips.

"What? How?" I cried.

Then they were gone.

"You're okay. You look normal now." Raz rubbed my shoulders, amusement and awe in his eyes. "Your eyes were changing colors, too. That was quite something but would've raised too many questions if anyone saw."

"I don't understand," I whispered, lowering a hand to my racing heart. "I can't shift, but Thembi said I can give the illusion that I do. It's like I feel Arjun's tiger becoming part of me."

"He's the one that would be able to tell you all about it," Raz assured.

"Well he's definitely in there," I said, turning toward the shipping containers. "I can barely feel the human part of him at all. He feels almost all tiger."

"Poor guy," Raz said sympathetically. "He stayed in that form while we were together to hide that he was a shifter. People thought it was weird for the lizard-man to get to attached to one of the tigers. He must've done the same thing this time."

"So they're not even bothering to treat him like a human." The acidic taste of disgust built up in my throat. We *had* to get him out of there.

"Not if they're keeping him in there." Raz's lip curled at the shipping containers. "No light, no fresh air. No wonder he's so miserable."

Feeling brazen, I approached the large metal box and drummed my fingers against the side. A soft vibration echoed back through my fingertips and my breath caught in my throat. That was no magic. Just the simple sensation of someone moving on the other side.

Yes, we're here! I wanted to yell against the metal wall. *We're going to get you out. Please don't give up.*

But I just drummed my fingers a few more times, hoping the gentle sound gave him a clue. I wondered if he could feel me like I felt him even when we weren't speaking.

Arjun? I tried.

No response. My projected thought went through what felt like a long, empty hallway.

"Are y'all lookin' for somethin'?"

We turned to see a man with an aged, weathered face approach us with suspicious, beady eyes. His clothes were covered in old paint and oil streaks, as if he was some kind of maintenance worker. What caught my eye was the thick, white bandage wrapped around his forearm.

Yes, I'd seen this man before. Through the bars of a cage.

"Hi!" I flashed him my plastered, young bimbo smile. "We're auditioning for jobs and just killing time while they get ready."

"Well, y'all can't be back here," he snarled, bringing his bandaged forearm close to his body. "This is where the animals are kept. It's dangerous."

"Oooh, what kind of animals do you have?" I widened my eyes as far as I could while raising my voice.

"Lots. We got show horses, goats, dogs, monkeys. One tiger and we got an elephant too."

"Wow, so cool!" I exclaimed, though my stomach twisted in on itself like a knot. Arjun was the only shifter I could sense here, but those other animals surely didn't have it any easier.

"Yeah, y'all need to git," he insisted, sweeping his good arm in a gesture for us to leave.

Raz and I followed his lead, but I couldn't help turning back and staring pointedly at his bandage.

"What happened to your arm?"

"Damn tiger took a swipe at me. He's a mean son of a bitch, but it's alright," the man sneered. "I'm gettin' 'im back this afternoon."

"Oh, what are you doing?"

The man raised his good arm and straightened it out in front of him, pointing his index finger and bending his thumb like aiming a gun. He closed one eye and smirked as he looked down his finger at me.

"I'm shooting that fucker and watching him bleed."

RAZVAN

"What are we gonna do?"

Mel paced back and forth furiously, her brow tense and furrowed. I tried not to let myself get distracted by her burlesque outfit—sheer stockings covering her long legs, an under-bust corset with a matching bra on top, and her skirt, which was little more than a mass of dark lace surrounding her hips.

Every time I enjoyed the view of her legs striding out as she walked, I remembered she would be shedding clothing for these dirty rednecks and it made me want to burn down this shitty tent we were in.

"We'll think of something, *steluța*," I murmured. "We still have some time."

"He said this afternoon! It's almost one now. What if they do it while we're auditioning? We'll have come undercover for nothing?"

"You'll be able to sense his distress," I assured her. "I can light something on fire and create a diversion. Then we'll go to him."

"But it might be too late by then!"

She was right, and despite doing my best to keep a level head and think things through, my mind was completely blank at how we would pull this off. I didn't have Connor's brashness or Hunter's calm, perceptive abilities. I just knew my way around sharp, pointy things and lighting fires.

Phil poked his head behind the curtain at us, or rather at Mel. He completely ignored my presence while his tongue practically wagged at her. I wanted to singe that thirsty look right off his face.

"We're ready for you, darlin'," he told her.

"Thanks." She flashed him a smile. I couldn't understand how she could fake looking so cheery. It had to be one of those hidden talents of women, putting on a brave face around men who disgusted them. "Start my music up?"

He nodded, and his shiny bald head disappeared. She moved to her position at the edge of the stage, took a deep breath, and swallowed.

"You don't have to do this, *steluţa*." My voice strained as I took hold of her arm. "Your presence on the stage is wasted on shit like this. You're capable of so much more."

"It's okay, Raz." She reached up and touched my cheek, those large brown eyes swallowing me up. "I have an idea. I'm going to see how much I can channel my ringmistress into this."

"I just hate to see you degraded. To see the things they want to do to you plainly on their faces."

She pressed a kiss to my mouth, her soft tongue surging between my lips in search of mine, which I happily gave to her.

"If this goes like I hope," she whispered. "They'll be just distracted enough for you to go and rescue Arjun."

"Mel!" I hissed in a whisper. "I'm not leaving you here."

"Watch their faces," she told me, one foot out in front of the curtain already. "When the time is right, you'll know."

With that, she released me and walked out into the spotlight.

The claps, cheers, and wolf whistles from the small audience of carnival staff made my heart sink. They were getting a free private show and probably had every intention of doing more with her immediately after. Just the thought of any of them touching her sent wisps of smoke coming from my mouth. Still, I did as she asked and watched.

Mel stepped gracefully onto the stage, waving, blowing kisses, and no doubt smiling. Unsurprisingly, they were entranced by her already.

Her hips swayed as she began her dance to a classic burlesque music pick, some kind of lounge ballad from the 1920s. Their eyes became glued to her form as her legs, hands, and hips did the talking. She articulated each point of her toe and curl of her finger, and they didn't miss any of it.

Dancing a slow circle around a three-legged stool in the middle of the stage, she was the ultimate tease and the perfect dream all at the same time. Taking a seat on the stool, her back arched and the angle at which she sat accentuated the curves of her legs and hips. Her fingers glided from her ankle to her upper thigh, where she began the slow, torturous tease of removing her stocking.

My jaw dropped as I watched her. I had no idea she

could do this. She watched the burlesque show back in Crying Falls maybe a handful of times. How could she emulate their movements so perfectly, if even better?

I blinked and quickly shook my head, feeling like I had tunnel vision while looking at her. Then I looked at the audience, and it hit me.

They were frozen like statues, all looking at her with wide-eyed, glazed expressions. No one moved or made a sound. Only their eyes tracked her movement.

My heart beat like a drum in my chest while adrenaline surged through my body. This was what she was talking about. As long as she performed, she had them captured and at her mercy. It could only be yet another aspect of her shaman abilities, but I didn't have time to speculate. I hurried off the stage and ran right past them. No one even noticed me.

I took off toward the shipping container we just visited. Pressing against the metal box, I made a slow circle around it. With a quick intention, I shifted just enough to sense vibrations in the air and through the ground to know if anyone was coming.

With the coast clear, I threw open the door and nearly retched at the smell that assaulted me from inside. Shit, piss, rotting flesh. All of it combined to make one of the foulest stenches I ever sensed, even from when I was captured.

Holding my breath, I jumped inside, still pressing myself to the wall.

"Arjun?" I whispered into the dark, rank prison. "You in here?"

I shifted a little more to gain my dragon's ability to see in the dark, and my heart sank. Among the scattered bones and half-rotting corpses of smaller animals strewn across the floor, only an empty cage greeted me at the far end of the shipping container.

"Fuck," I hissed and turned toward the exit, running my fingers across my scalp. What now? I could sense shifters when they were close to me, but I didn't have Mel's tracking abilities. I couldn't sense his location and hone in on him like she could.

I jumped down from the shipping container, feeling the ripples of vibrations up through my feet, and paused. Maybe...

Holding my breath, I focused hard. I could feel the footsteps of every human for miles around. The air across my skin gave me a blueprint of their movement. I was looking for four heavy steps, not two.

Come on, Arjun, where are you... there!

The air tasted thick with human sweat and fear, mixed with the odd-smelling pheromones of a big cat I only knew from the memory of being in such close quarters with Arjun before. Four sets of light human footsteps stumbled and pulled, trying to move the massive four-legged animal to somewhere he didn't want to go.

I followed the scent of human fear and the vibrations on the ground, which led me on a zigzagging trail behind all the shipping containers and defunct equipment at the back of the carnival. Of course, they wouldn't drag him through the main strip. They didn't want to be seen taking an endangered animal to its slow, painful death.

Angry voices and feline growls floated up to reach my still-human ears, and I ducked behind a pile of shipping pallets. They were just on the other side and, if I wasn't mistaken, just a few feet away from the small stage where Mel had the carnival staff under a spell.

Could she sense him nearby while casting her magic onstage? And could he sense her?

Arjun's growls and roars became louder, more savage and bloodthirsty. I realized he could possibly smell me, too. Would he remember my scent?

"Jesus, let's just knock him out already!" one of the humans demanded.

"Fuck no! I want him conscious when I get my shots in!" I recognized that voice as the man with the bandaged arm.

"Dumbass cocksucker, we're gonna get mauled to death before we even make it to the shooting range!"

While they argued, I saw no better opportunity and climbed on top of the shipping pallets.

"Arjun, run!" I screamed before shifting my lungs and sucking in a big breath of oxygen. The humans only had time to turn around and look at me before getting consumed by the massive ball of fire erupting from my mouth.

The blast sent them reeling back, releasing the chains around Arjun's neck and forcing them to the ground, where they rolled around with panicked, desperate screams to put themselves out.

Arjun took off in a flash of orange fur—straight toward the back of the stage where Mel was performing.

"Wait!" I hollered as I jumped to the ground and ran after him. "The shaman! Don't hurt her!" But I didn't need to worry.

He scrambled up the small stairs meant for human legs and darted past the curtain. I caught up just in time to see him leap past Mel and sail straight into the crowd as if in slow motion. He looked magnificent for the split second he hovered in midair. Twelve feet long from head to tail, claws stretched out and on deadly display. Such a massive animal weighing hundreds of pounds with the natural abilities of feline grace and lightness.

The moment he fell, sinking his claws and teeth into the unsuspecting human's fleshy body, the spell was broken.

Mel was forgotten onstage as screams and chaos rang out. People fell over their chairs and each other as they tried to run, but one swipe of Arjun's paw left them incapacitated. The smell of blood filled the air as I jumped onstage and grabbed Mel.

"We have to go," I told her. "Now!"

"He's on a rampage," she cried, eyes wide in shock at the horror in front of us. "I don't know how to stop him."

"You're a shaman, talk to him," I said, pulling her off the stage to the side. "Make him follow us, but we can't stay here!"

She nodded, following me backstage and through the maze of trailers, pallets, and shipping containers behind the carnival.

"He's not answering," she said, her voice rising in panic. "I'm yelling his name but it's like no one's home."

"Talk to his tiger, then," I said, pulling her along behind me. "You can feel what the animal feels and emulate it. Do that."

I hopped in my truck and turned it on, my foot hovering over the gas pedal as she climbed robotically in next to me. Her face wore a vacant look before I saw the flickers of tiger-like features appear. Her eyes turned a pale yellowish-green, followed by her canine teeth elongating past her lower lip.

"Mel," I said harshly. "We can't wait for him. We're fucked if we stay sitting here."

"I know, I'm trying," she answered in despair. "Just a little longer—"

Right then, a massive orange shape came loping out past the carnival trailers. In the next instant, my truck bed sagged from the weight of Arjun jumping in.

"That's it, let's go!" Mel cried. She turned and opened the rear window. "Arjun, lay down!"

The Bengal tiger met her eyes as he reclined down below the edges of my truck bed and I peeled out of there with the pedal to the floor.

12

CONNOR

"We're not in Kansas anymore, Toto," I muttered, looking out the passenger window at the lush greenery surrounding us.

"Dog jokes. So original," Hunter scoffed next to me.

"I honestly didn't mean it like that," I laughed. "There's just no other way to describe this place, aside from entering the Twilight Zone, maybe."

The complete opposite of Fulmer and the rest of the dried out, rundown parts of Georgia we'd seen, the nonprofit center shone like an oasis. Manicured lawns, carefully trimmed topiaries, and trellises with climbing vines surrounded us.

"It is... something," Hunter observed eloquently.

I looked at him. "I know you're just as worried about Mel as I am, but keep your head in the game, bro. I don't trust shiny-ass places like this. It creeps me out more than the ghetto carnival we left them at."

"Not just Mel," he admitted. "I'm worried about both of them."

Oh, right. I never had deep feelings for anyone but women, so I momentarily forgot about the flame he carried for Razvan, too.

"They'll be fine," I told him. "She's gonna be a pain in his ass but she's resourceful too." Despite myself, I checked my phone for the hundredth time. Still no call. I could only assume no news was good news.

The acres of perfect lawns finally ended and Hunter parked the RV in a nearly empty parking lot in front of a pristine white building. When we got out and I settled my ass in the wheelchair for hopefully the last time, I rolled up to the front entrance to see the words *FDR Center for Disabled Veterans* painted on the door.

"After you." Hunter pulled the door open for me, his pups clinging to his side as they blinked up at the massive, sterile building. They'd probably never seen anything like it.

I wheeled through, my tires barely making a sound over the cool tile floor. Hunter's footsteps echoed off the walls as he followed me in.

"Good afternoon," the attractive middle-aged woman at the front desk greeted me with one-hundred percent southern charm. "How can I help y'all?"

"My name's Connor Shaw," I told her. "I was told Dr. Selow would be expecting me."

"Of course, hun. I'll take you right to his office." She glanced past me at Hunter and the kids. "Would y'all care to wait here? The executive director would like to talk to Mr. Shaw privately."

"Sure." Hunter shot her a friendly smile and took a seat

on one of the couches, the only thing with softness and no hard edges in the room.

"Help yourselves to tea or coffee," the receptionist told him as she rose from her desk. "Follow me, Mr. Shaw."

I wheeled slowly past Hunter. "I'm tellin' you, he's gonna harvest my kidneys," I muttered. "Or bend me over his desk. I'm not sure which is worse."

"I'll listen for the screams," he snorted, picking up a magazine. "Or moans of pleasure. You never know."

"Funny, wolf-man," I muttered. "Oh, here." I tossed him my cell phone. "In case Mel calls."

I followed Dr. Selow's receptionist past several people working at desks in an open office area. A large window on one side looked into some kind of gym or physical therapy room. Some people worked out on machines like normal. Others, mostly amputees, practiced balance or with resistance bands with trainers standing by.

She pushed open a large wooden door at the far end of the room and stepped aside to let me in.

"Mr. Shaw here to see you, sir," she announced chirpily.

"Thank you, Margaret. I'll take it from here."

As she left, I wheeled up to the large mahogany desk to get a closer look at the man who was apparently so interested in me.

He was in his forties with salt and pepper hair, dressed business casual in a polo and slacks, as he rounded the desk to greet me. And he looked startlingly familiar.

"Connor." he approached me with a smile and his hand out. "It's so good to see you again! Damn, how many years has it been?"

"Too many for me to remember, it seems," I answered,

giving his hand a tentative shake. "I know your face, but I can't place from where."

The smile fell, turning his friendly expression into a mask of concern. "You don't remember how you know me? Do you recognize my name?"

I lowered my eyes to the nameplate on his desk, which read *Dr. Brian R. Selow - Executive Director*.

"No, man. Sorry."

He nodded, clenching his jaw and folding his arms as he leaned against his desk. "I see. Can you tell me what you remember about losing your legs?"

I sighed. "Not much. Look, man. Whatever history we may or may not have doesn't matter to me. I was told you can help. I need legs to work and provide for my family. Can you fit me with some or not?"

I swallowed a lump in my throat, but lifted my chin with pride. Mel, Raz, Hunter, and the pups were probably the most misfitted, wackiest family out there, but that was truly how I saw us at this point. I had my love-hate relationship with performing, but I'd earn my keep for all of us. I refused to be dead weight.

"Do you remember the unit you were with?" Dr. Selow continued. "The faces and names of the people you saved?"

Damn it. He really wasn't going to let this go.

"I didn't save anyone," I replied. "All I remember is mangled body parts strewn across the desert. I shouldn't have lived, myself. But I dragged myself a couple miles toward our checkpoint while terrorists laughed and threw shit at me. They didn't even bother shooting because they figured I'd be dead once the vultures got to me."

"But you *did* save people, Connor," he insisted, lowering his voice to a whisper. "You stopped the blast from hitting our medic vehicle en route to the checkpoint. Sargent Kelly Armstrong. Lieutenant Andrew Malkin. And me. Captain Brian Selow, US Marine doctor."

A memory struggled to surface. A man with a face much like Dr. Selow's but younger, with less gray. He injected a needle into my arm. My legs swung back and forth—legs that still wore boots on my feet—as he jokingly slapped a Sesame Street bandaid over the injection spot.

"Did you... give me a flu shot?"

"Yes!" The smile returned to the current Dr. Selow's face. "The morning of the blast. Your trauma must have kept you from retaining certain memories, Connor. But I was there, brother. You saved me, and two others."

I let out a long breath, desperately trying to locate other memories, as he picked up a picture frame from his desk and showed it to me.

"Because of you, I got to return home to my wife and little girl." His voice choked as he looked down at the smiling woman hugging her daughter. "My daughter didn't have to grow up without a father. You have a family too, you must know what that feels like."

I didn't bother correcting him. The importance of this meeting became clear in an instant.

"After our unit pulled out, I searched high and low to find you," he continued. "You were declared Missing in Action for a moment, but then found. After that, it seemed like you discharged and disappeared for good."

"I did, in a sense." The answer came out gruff. I wasn't used to being treated like a hero. "The VA could only spend so many precious resources on me, so I found my own way."

"Oh, believe me, I've had it up to here with the VA," Dr. Selow scoffed. "That's why I put everything I had into making this place. I figured if I couldn't find you, I'd dedicate my retirement to helping other heroes like you."

"I'm no hero," I argued with a shake of my head. "Just some guy the universe likes to fuck with."

"You are," he insisted. "And for your service to this country, for what you've lost and endured, you deserve financial and lifestyle compensation. That's what this place is all about." He shook his head with a small laugh. "I thought I was hallucinating when Dr. Harman called me. I told him to repeat your name like ten times. The universe works in funny ways."

"Look, Doc," I said. "I'm not a supersentimental guy, but say I believe you. What's next? What can this place do for me? I don't mean to be so cut and dry, but I gotta get back out there."

"Of course." Dr. Selow rounded his desk again. "We can get you tested and fitted for new prosthetics immediately. Are you also in need of PTSD therapy?"

"Yes," I said through gritted teeth, knowing Mel would insist on it.

"How about housing?"

"Can you fit four adults and two kids?" I asked, half-jokingly. "We're living out of two vehicles currently."

"Absolutely. We have houses with up to six bedrooms right here on campus," he shrugged. "Some military folks have large families."

The smile dropped from my face. "You serious? How much does that cost?"

"To you? Nothing," he grinned. "All services here are funded by grants and donations, Connor."

"Goddamn." A small glimmer of hope lit up within my chest. It had been years since I slept in an actual house. We wouldn't stay here forever, of course, but a real house with bedrooms? How much would Mel love that?

"And there's no catch? No price at all?" I asked, refusing to let go of my skepticism.

Dr. Selow's eyes dropped to my legs, one of which ended just below my knee and the other halfway down my shin.

"I'd say you've paid enough of a price already," he answered quietly. "I'd be just as bad as the government if I were to ask you for more."

Logically, I knew he was right. Injured veterans deserved so much more than what they got upon returning home. Still, I hated receiving charity. I hated the pitying looks while I was homeless more than the looks of disgust. That was why I chose to work instead and hid my disability from those I didn't trust.

My pride or whatever didn't want to be included in the label "disabled veteran", and therefore entitled to receive services from non-profits like these. But then I thought of Mel, and how much my stubbornness hurt her already. She'd stick by me no matter what, but I needed to put aside my own pride and make her proud. She deserved a man worthy of her, and if she insisted on sticking by me, I'd make sure to be that man for her.

"I guess you got yourself a deal."

"Great!" Dr. Selow beamed at me. "We'll get you enrolled with our physical therapists tomorrow. I'll call the groundskeeper now and see about getting a house cleaned and ready for y—"

A loud bang startled us both. I wheeled around to see

Hunter striding toward me, a serious look on his face and Dr. Selow's receptionist trailing behind him.

"I'm sorry, doctor," she cried. "I told him not to barge in but—"

"It's Raz," Hunter held out the phone to me, the screen indicating he was in the middle of a call. "They just got out, but they're in trouble. They need us."

13

MELODY

"Arjun." I made my voice as soothing as possible. "Can you please shift to human? This would be a lot easier if you were in human form."

The tiger flattened his ears against his skull and growled a low warning at me. His tail whipped threateningly back and forth in the truck bed.

"Shhh, okay!" I waved my hands frantically. "Just no growling or tail-whipping."

I looked up at Razvan, his ear still attached to the pay phone receiver outside the grocery store where we parked.

We had zigzagged all through town with a massive tiger in his truck bed, hoping to shake off the carnival people in case they followed us. Neither of us saw any, thankfully. They might have been too busy treating their injured or not willing to chase an animal they were going to kill anyway, but I kept looking around for anyone who might have followed us.

Now, in the next town over, we stopped to call Connor and figure out what to do next. My mind was at a loss for a plan for once. Getting Arjun out had been easy, relatively speaking. Now that we had him, we had no idea what to do with him.

On top of that, he never answered when I spoke to him telepathically and refused to shift to human. It would be one thing to drive around with a naked man in the truck, but something else entirely to hide a five-hundred pound striped cat.

Finally, Raz hung up the phone and started back toward me.

"We're going to them," he said, pulling open the driver's side door. "Apparently Connor has a house now."

"What?" I looked at Arjun. "You're gonna have to get down again."

The tiger lowered his head to his paws, his feline eyes wide and bright on me before I jumped back up front with Raz.

"A six-bedroom, fully furnished house for the injured soldier and his large family," he chuckled. "Feels like we hit the jackpot."

"That's great and all, but what are we going to do about him?" I pointed out the back window where the tiger laid low. "I'm pretty sure they'll object to us bringing a tiger to a house owned by this place."

"He still won't shift?"

"Won't shift, won't talk, nothing," I cried in exasperation. "I can't get through to him at all. It's all tiger I feel."

"He must've been in animal form too long," he muttered. "The human side of him has grown weak and lost control."

"How do I get the human side of him back?"

"I don't know if you can, shaman," he glanced over at me apologetically.

Arjun wouldn't fit in the trailer we pulled full of Raz's stuff, so our next best option was covering him with a tarp and praying nobody at the organization would want to inspect our truck. The tiger thankfully didn't object too harshly when we stopped and laid the tarp over him. A few growls and teeth-baring, but he allowed me to drape the material over his head and body.

"He hasn't attacked us," I observed as Raz and I climbed back up front. "Which means he's not acting entirely like a wild animal. He must know we're not going to hurt him, so Arjun the human must still have some control."

"I really hope you're right, *steluța*," he said quietly. "I'd love to be able to talk to my friend again."

A few miles later, we drove onto the nonprofit grounds, which looked more like a resort than a center for disabled veterans. A smiling groundskeeper waved us through without making any motions to stop or inspect the truck. I released the breath I'd been holding as we drove around the pristine white building and entered what looked like a suburban neighborhood behind it.

"Con said keep going straight toward the back," Raz muttered. "They're waiting for us."

"I hope they have a plan to keep this big cat hidden," I muttered back.

The landscape turned more wild and rural the further back we went. It reminded me a bit of the forest surrounding the Crying Falls festival. I had to admit I'd grown attached to that place. I missed the fresh pine smell in the air, cooking over campfires, the starry sky and all the memories in those woods. Meeting Hunter for the first time, seeing Raz shift under the moonlight, and feeling the wild energy as I commanded the stage.

"Holy shit," Raz breathed.

"Oh, my god!" I brought a hand to my mouth in shock.

It was a gorgeous, two-story plantation house with a wraparound porch, set back amongst the trees with plenty of privacy and space. I couldn't believe my eyes. This place was *ours?*

Two wolf pups wrestled on the massive lawn, which seemed to stretch on forever. When we pulled up, they yipped and howled as they ran alongside us. Roo and Rinna never looked so happy and playful before. They looked at peace, at home.

"Welcome home, you two," Hunter greeted us from the porch, his golden eyes passing over both of us affectionately.

"What do you mean, home?" I asked hesitantly as I stepped out of the truck. "Surely, we can't actually stay here?"

"We can for as long as I'm using the center's services." Connor wheeled up next to Hunter as Raz and I approached them in a daze.

"But how?"

"Oh, the director is definitely pulling some strings since none of us are married," he smirked. "But I apparently saved his life years ago, so he's happy to do it."

"Apparently?"

He nodded. "I don't remember it. Not well. But the blast that ruined my legs narrowly missed him and a couple other people, thanks to me taking most of it."

"So..." I looked up at the house, the likes of which I'd

only seen before in magazines. I never even walked through a neighborhood and saw houses like these in real life, let alone lived in one. "This is really ours?"

"It is, babe." Connor reached forward and squeezed my hands. "Maybe not forever, but I'm constantly a work in progress so we'll see."

"So they're treating your pain? And getting you new prosthetics?"

"That and more," he smiled up at me. "You deserve nothing less than a house like this and a man who strives to be better every day for you."

"Connor..."

I barely had time to wrap my arms around his neck and kiss him when Raz and Hunter started yelling in a panic.

"Kids, come here!" Hunter screamed at the top of his lungs. "Watch out for the tiger."

"Shit!"

I whipped around to see a blur of orange race across the lawn toward the trees surrounding the house.

"Con, keep the kids close!" I instructed. "Raz, Hunter, let's go after him."

The shifters followed closely behind me as I started in the direction where Arjun ran.

"Be careful, he's in hunting mode," I said, sensing the wave of bloodthirst from him through our shared connection. He hadn't hunted properly in so long. I could feel his desire to sink his teeth into soft, warm flesh and feel the hot trickle of blood across his tongue...

I shook my head. *Snap out of it, Mel.* I couldn't afford to lose myself to the sensations that already ruled him.

"He went this way," Hunter pointed. "He's not far."

"He's not moving," Razvan said after a few minutes of

walking in the direction Hunter pointed. "He's just staying in one place. What's he—"

"There!" I pointed to about twenty feet ahead of us, where a naked man with dark hair and caramel skin tore into the limp carcass of a bird with his bare hands.

The three of us froze, unsure what to do. Arjun had shifted to human at some point but still tore into his prey like an animal.

"Let me," Razvan muttered, approaching him slowly.

Arjun paused and looked up at the tattooed man coming toward him with wide, multicolored eyes. His nose, cheeks, lips, chin, and chest were smeared with blood and bird guts, but Razvan paid no mind to his appearance as he smiled at his old friend.

"Hey mate," he greeted softly. "You remember me, don't you?"

The tiger shifter bared his human teeth and inhaled deeply.

"Yeah, you know I smell familiar, you big pussy cat," Razvan smirked and held an arm out to me. "This is Melody, the shaman who spoke to you. It's all because of her we got you out, man. You can hunt, be a cat or a human freely now. You don't have to touch fire anymore. You're free."

Arjun turned his gaze to me. Even with dead bird entrails smeared all over him, he was strikingly handsome. Those eyes looked straight to my soul.

"Melody? The shaman?" he breathed, a light English accent peppering his words.

"Yes, Arjun." I approached him with slow, careful steps, just as Raz had. "You're not in danger anymore. We're here to help you."

He held my gaze for a long moment where no one seemed to breathe, then stood to his full height. I kept my focus on his face, nearly at the same level as Hunter's. Like my pale wolf, his musculature was long, slender and graceful, only covered in warm, coppery skin with a dusting of dark hair on his chest.

Razvan swiftly removed his shirt and tied it around Arjun's hips to give him some sense of modesty. My face flamed at the realization that my eyes had been traveling lower down his sculpted body. He didn't need anyone ogling him right now.

"Come on, mate," Raz wrapped an arm around the naked man's waist and draped one of his arms over his shoulders. "Let's get you inside. Bet you haven't felt a bed in a long while, ah?"

With Razvan's support, Arjun took a few wobbly steps as if he hadn't used his human legs in ages. Only when we came out of the forest and reached the lawn did I notice the burn scars all over his feet. Now out from under the cover of the trees, I saw his hands and ribs carried the same scars.

"He's okay now." Hunter rubbed the nape of my neck reassuringly. "Or he will be, at least."

"We can't keep doing this." My own voice sounded far away. "They'll just replace him with another. And when that shifter drops dead, they'll just get another. We have to stop this for good. What can we do, Hunter?"

"I'm not sure, little fox," he replied sadly. "It's shocking to you, but we've been aware of these dangers our whole lives. Human entertainment is just another predator we have to look out for, and sometimes fall victim to."

"It shouldn't be," I argued. "And what about those like

Raz who never knew any other shifters? They just think they're human until they start sprouting tails and fur or horns."

"Again, I don't know the answer to that."

I moved away from him, speed walking up to Arjun's other side to help Raz get him into the house. I wasn't angry at Hunter, just at the hopelessness of the situation. I didn't expect him to have the answers but there had to be another besides, *I don't know*, and, *we just deal with this*.

"*Steluța*, go in and draw a bath for him. Then help me get him cleaned up." Raz craned his neck around Arjun's arm to address Hunter. "See about making some food in the kitchen, would ya, wolf?"

"Sure."

Hunter and I ran inside ahead of him to do our assigned jobs. Once Raz and Arjun caught up to me in the bathroom, the tiger shifter's eyes lit up when he saw the water running in the tub and practically pounced in.

"I forgot how much these cats actually like water," Razvan chuckled.

As Arjun splashed his face and hair joyously, I made a silent promise to end the cruel trade that did this to him, Razvan, and Hunter. I may have been the last shaman left, but every human alive who raised a hand to a shifter would soon learn my name.

14

HUNTER

My ears pricked at the sound of light footsteps behind me, moving softly but still too heavy to be Mel's. My heartbeat quickened at the smoky, wild smell that accompanied those steps.

"How'd he like the food?" I asked Raz without turning away from the sink.

"Devoured it all. I suppose he was hungry," he laughed, setting the bowls next to me on the counter. "I'll wash these."

"No, it's okay. I got it." I kept my eyes focused on the soapy water in front of me, my hands scrubbing vigorously. "Where's Mel?"

"On a tour with Connor. They're exploring the grounds before he starts treatment tomorrow."

"And your tiger friend?"

"Sleeping. I expect he'll be out for a good eighteen hours or so," he chuckled, shaking his head as he turned to lean his back against the counter. He stood so close his arm nearly brushed mine. "Cats, you know how they are.

Hope you and him don't chase each other like a couple of domestic pets."

"I have no intention of chasing an animal over twice my size," I scoffed. "When it comes to him or me, there's no question of who would win."

"Oh? Have you gone humble on me, alpha?" Raz smacked my arm playfully with the back of his hand.

That touch, along with his use of the word *alpha*, sent heat and hardness running from my chest straight to my cock. Jesus, why did he have to affect me like this? Why couldn't Mel be enough for me?

"I'm not an alpha," I replied. "At least, I never got that opportunity."

"No?" I still didn't tear my attention away from the dishes, but I could see his face in my mind. One eyebrow cocked, gray eyes looking at me and waiting, like he expected an actual answer.

"My former mate was our alpha's daughter," I explained. "When she chose me, we were expected to become the new pack leaders. She was killed, and then I was captured before that could happen."

"Well, you're sort of the alpha now." I could see his smirk in my mind. "You're with the head female after all."

"Yeah, but so are you," I answered. "So's Connor. This whole situation hasn't exactly created a hierarchy between us."

"You're right, it hasn't," he said softly. "Does that confuse you?"

"No," I replied. "I feel like I know my place with her. You?"

"Yeah, same," he said in a soft voice. "I'm not jealous of

anyone because I know what I mean to her, and what she means to me."

"Right," I agreed, turning to put plates on the drying rack and wipe my hands on a towel. "Same here."

The air was so thick with tension between us, I could barely breathe. I wanted to move away, to get space and hopefully get my goddamn cock to calm down. But his hand on my shoulder, the weight and heat of it, made me stop.

"Why are we dancing in circles around this, wolf?" Raz's voice was thick and husky. "Why not just be open about what's going on?"

"Look, Raz," I brushed his hand off of me and turned to face him, meeting his eyes for the first time since he walked into the kitchen. "It's not that easy, okay?"

"Why not?" he challenged. "No one's going to object. Mel knows. She wants us to embrace this. She just wants us to be happy."

"Because I grew up around humans too," I retorted. "Not far from here. And this," I gestured between us, "is wrong. I've been taught my whole life that being with another man in the same way as a woman is wrong. Haven't you ever seen that?"

"Hunter," he scoffed, crossing his arms. "I've been told my very existence is wrong from the moment I breathed fire for the first time at five years old. At least you had a community of other shifters like you. Me? I was told I was a curse. A punishment on my family because I couldn't control the scales growing on my skin. Fucking another man? That's the least of my sins."

I couldn't stop staring at how his biceps bulged. My

gaze drifted down as his words sank in and my pulse shot up when I realized he was just as hard as me.

Fuck! I tore my eyes away. He must've caught me looking. Couldn't he see how difficult this was for me?

"What about Mel?" I said, my voice thick with desire I didn't want to feel. "Even if she says she's okay with this, her mind could change if it actually happens. I don't want to make her uncomfortable, ever."

"Neither do I," he said with a nod of his head. "So if you want to mess around, we'll only proceed when she's involved. Simple."

I nodded my agreement, relief lifting off my shoulders until the moment he stepped into my space, grinning.

"Does that mean you *do* want to mess around?"

"No." My protest was weak, and he saw right through it. "I—"

"Hunter."

He touched me again, a deliberate caress along my ribs until his hand rested on my back. It was nothing like a woman's touch, but still *so* good. Strong, firm, and warm. I knew exactly how strong he was, and it excited me just as much as Mel's softness.

"You liked playing in the pool with me," he breathed, stepping in closer until his chest barely brushed mine. "You wanted to keep going until we collapsed."

"That wasn't like this."

"Don't kid yourself, alpha." His arm tightened around me, pulling himself against me until I felt his own racing heart across from mine. "Mel saw the whole thing, and she was so fucking turned on, Connor got her off with just his hand. If I tried to kiss you then, would you have refused me?"

I couldn't answer. My voice didn't seem to work as his other arm came to wrap around me.

"You don't have to fight it." He nudged his nose just under my chin, his warm breath fanning across my throat. "This is who you are, Hunter. Mel, Connor, and I all accept you."

His lips grazed my neck. I wanted to lean into them, to feel that split tongue that seemed to please Mel so much against my throat. I even let out a soft groan as he paused, not fully kissing me, just hovering his mouth on my neck. But years of buried shame couldn't be erased that easily.

"Raz, stop."

I pulled away, needing to put as much distance between me and the dragon shifter as possible. Stumbling out onto the porch from that hot stuffy kitchen, a run to clear my head seemed to be just what I needed.

"Hey."

I turned my head to see Connor and Mel approaching the house, curious looks on both of their faces.

"You alright?" she asked amusedly. Her eyes dropped to my waist, where I knew my erection remained at full strength. Damn, I stayed in that kitchen way too long.

"Yeah," I answered as casually as I could muster. "Just going for a run. Would you let the kids know for me?"

"Sure. You want them with you?"

"No, that's okay." I peeled off my shirt and placed it over the railing of the porch for when I'd return. "I'm going solo." My hand drifted to the button of my jeans. I didn't want to take my pants off until Mel was inside.

"Okay. Have fun."

They went in and I couldn't shift fast enough. I raced through the trees, light as a feather on my four paws. Birds and rodents scattered at my footsteps, but I wasn't hungry for them. I ran like I was trying to get something out of my system.

At the back of my mind, I knew I'd have to go back. I wasn't ready yet, but at some point I'd have to face not only him, but the person *I* was.

15

MELODY

To say Razvan looked guilty when Connor and I came home was an understatement.

"I don't suppose you have anything to do with Hunter running off into the woods with a raging hard-on, do you?"

"Who, me?" he brought his hands to his chest in feigned innocence. "You wound me, *steluța*."

"You can't come onto him too strong," Connor added, wheeling himself through the house. "He may be a shifter, but he's also a good ol' southern boy. He's got a lot of shame around having feelings for another man."

"Don't I know it," Razvan muttered. "I didn't come on *that* strongly but yeah, maybe spooked him a little."

"Leave him alone when he gets back," I jabbed my index finger into his chest. "He won't come to you if you keep spooking him. You've got to give him space."

"And who am I supposed to harass in the meantime?" His eyes flashed excitedly right before he lunged forward, grabbed me by the waist, and covered my face and neck with kisses.

"Raz!" I squealed, wriggling in his arms, which just egged him on. He tickled my sides and kissed me everywhere, torturing me mercilessly until I could barely breathe.

"Hey, have you guys checked this place out?" Connor called from somewhere in the house, his voice echoing off the high, slanted ceilings.

"I'm trying, but Raz won't let me go!"

The dragon released me to arm's length before he snapped out a hand, grabbed me, and pulled me back in. He just chuckled at my weak muttered protests, his feet following my steps toward Connor's voice while wrapped around me like a snake around its prey.

"Whoa." I stopped at the entryway and even Raz had to look up at the room laid out before us.

A TV screen took up nearly one entire wall, with half a dozen deep comfortable recliners facing the screen a few feet away. Shelves lined the walls, filled with Blu-ray and DVD movies of every genre imaginable.

On the other side of the room, a half-wall sectioned off a smaller area with a loveseat, an armchair, and bookshelves stacked with books. My fingers squeezed around Raz's at the thought of curling up with a book in a cozy, peaceful corner.

"Man, imagine watching the football games in here!" Connor spun in his wheelchair excitedly.

"I don't really watch American football," Raz admitted.

"Ah, Christ. You foreigners don't get it. Babe?"

I shook my head. "Not really into it. Sorry, babe."

"Damn it! *This* is why you can't scare Hunter away, Raz.

I need a good ol' American boy to yell at the screen with me."

So much for cozy and peaceful.

"You guys want to watch a movie until he gets back?" I let go of Raz's hand to browse the shelves.

"Sure, but no war movies." Connor's face turned serious, and I shot him a sympathetic look. My finger skimmed past Black Hawk Down, Saving Private Ryan, and similar titles.

"You don't think we'll wake up Arjun?" I asked, pausing my browsing to look over at Raz.

"Nah, he's out like a light." My dragon came up next to me to browse more movie titles. "We probably won't see him until tomorrow morning."

We settled on Snatch, which I'd never seen, but both of the guys loved and told me I had to see it. Raz found some microwave popcorn in the kitchen and soon, two of my three men sank into the recliners on either side of me for our movie experience.

I propped my feet up in Connor's lap, relishing in the firmness of his fingers massaging into my arches. Raz held the bowl of popcorn and fed it to me, when I wasn't grabbing handfuls to feed Connor.

We munched and watched and laughed. I felt so blissfully happy, I couldn't wipe the grin off my face. It took me a moment to realize this was normal. As normal as my life could get, anyway. But this was what normal people did—watch movies with their loved ones without a care in the world.

I snuggled down lower into my recliner, stretching my legs across Connor and leaning my head on the armrest where Raz stroked my hair. I wanted to sink deep into this happiness like a bath and never leave. It wrapped around me like a blanket and I wanted to take it everywhere with me. Blissful normality. This was what I always wanted.

Not long after the popcorn ran out, the guys seemed to have other ideas.

Connor's foot massages turned into gentle stroking of my calves, which gradually reached higher up my legs. His fingers teased the sensitive skin of my inner thighs, sending my pulse racing as I tried to focus on the movie.

His light, teasing caresses became firm, kneading of my flesh, making my breath hitch. Raz tilted my chin up to make me look up at him from the armrest.

"Ever make out with a boy in a movie theater before?"

I shook my head, and then his mouth descended on me with a passionate kiss. While his tongue sent my heart racing, his hands slid into my bra cups while Connor handled my lower body. My shorts and underwear came away from my hips while I laid stretched out between them.

Kisses covered my inner thighs, my neck, my nipples. Then Connor covered the center of my heat with his mouth, and Razvan swallowed the moan that came from me.

The movie went on, nothing but background noise and light casting across our bodies. My guys had stripped me bare, but they still wore too many clothes. I reached for Razvan's shirt, only to have my wrists pinned down as his laughter floated across my skin.

"Greedy girl," he teased. "Isn't she, Con?"

"Mm-hm," my soldier agreed from between my thighs. He pressed a finger inside me, his lips pulling back into a smile at my gasping reaction. "She's so wet. She wants to come already. But we're not going to give it to you that easy, babe."

"Did you two plan this?" I panted, looking up at their pleased faces.

"You were so entranced by the movie, it was adorable," Raz grin. "You didn't even notice us mouthing at each other right above your head."

"Sneaky bastards," I grumbled.

Raz only laughed at my pout and pried my lips open with his tongue. I swore with that split down the middle, it was even stronger than a normal tongue. Connor returned to making my pussy feel like heaven, and soon I forgot all about being annoyed.

He pinned my hip down with a strong hand to keep me from thrashing, his tongue lashing mercilessly at my clit while his finger teased me with only a fraction of the fullness I'd soon be feeling.

"So fucking beautiful." Razvan trailed his lips down my throat, his hands running across my body and breasts until that tongue reached my nipples. Each side thrashed against the sensitive peaks until they hardened like pebbles. Their sensitivity made me cry out when he grazed his teeth against them.

"She's close, Con," he murmured to my other lover against my skin. "God, I love watching her come."

Connor moaned an unintelligible reply, his voice sending vibrations through me as he carried on tirelessly. My breaths became ragged, my hands flailed along the recliner, desperate for something to grab onto. That happened to be Razvan.

My fingers bunched around the soft, worn denim of his

pants, gripping hard and practically yanking them off his hips.

"Easy, girl," he teased, his tongue flicking the shell of my ear. "You'll have that pretty little pussy stuffed with cock in no time. Would you like that?"

Those words and the last few lashes of Connor's tongue sent me hurtling over the edge. My back arched off the seat just as Connor curled his fingers inside me, prolonging my pleasure. I thrashed like a madwoman and mewled like a kitten. Both guys stared in awe, running their hands across me and kissing me as the aftershocks made me shiver.

"Damn, I've never seen anything as gorgeous as that," Connor murmured, kissing my hip bones.

"Same here," Raz agreed, lifting me up so my head could rest on his chest.

"You guys..." I panted, reaching an arm up to wrap around Raz's neck.

"Yes?" Connor chuckled, laying his head on my thigh to look up at me adoringly. "Were you going to finish that thought?"

"I forgot what I was going to say."

The two of them laughed, with Connor looking as proud as a peacock.

"Just wait until it's my turn." Raz kissed sensually just under my ear. "You'll forget your own name."

"Oh, now it's a contest, huh?" Connor grinned. "Next time, babe, I'll make you forget the first letter of the alphabet."

The two of them traded boasts back and forth, growing more ridiculous every time until I wiped tears away from laughing so hard. When a door slammed in the kitchen, my laughter cut off abruptly and I peered over the top of the chairs.

"Hunter!" I called. "You're home."

"Um, yeah." The wolf paused at the entrance to the theater room, his pants low on his hips and unbuttoned as if he just pulled them on haphazardly. Carrying his t-shirt in his hand, his bare upper body flexed with deep breaths and glistened with a light sheen of sweat.

"Have a good run?" I asked, my pulse quickening.

"Yeah." His eyebrow quirked up at the sight of my bare shoulders over the tops of the chairs, as if he knew exactly what we were doing. "I was just going to shower." He turned, heading for the stairs.

"Wait."

He turned back, golden eyes already fired up. If he ran off to ease sexual tension between him and Razvan, it didn't work. Rather, it amplified it. Sweaty, tense, and breathing heavily, he looked like sex on legs. And in my current state of just coming under Connor's tongue, I wasn't going to let him walk away.

I placed both hands on the back of my chair, rising up to kneeling so he could see me from the waist up. His eyes dilated at the sight of me, no doubt taking in the redness of Raz's handprints marking my skin. My nipples pebbled again just from his lustful gaze.

I reached a hand out, a playful smile teasing at my lips.

"Come join us, Hunter."

16

MELODY

Hunter stayed rooted to his spot, neither coming closer nor moving away. Only his eyes moved, flickering from me to Razvan, then back to me.

"I won't touch you if you don't want me to. It can be just like the first time," Raz broke the silence, wrapping an arm around my waist. "But our girl wants to have fun with all of us."

That seemed to ease Hunter's nerves. His gaze returned to me as he stalked forward. Even in human form, he was so wolflike. Like prey, I froze—caught in a predator's trap until he stood right in front of me. His handsome mouth tipped up into a smirk as he cupped my face and kissed me.

His mouth devoured mine hungrily—more evidence that his run did nothing to diminish his desire, but only enhanced it. My hands slid down his long, lean torso, carving out the shape of his abs with my fingertips until I reached the waistband of his pants. He let out a soft growl as I shoved them down his thighs, breaking our kiss only to step out of them.

"Come here," I requested, my voice a breathy whisper.

He obliged, eyes locked on me as he came around the chairs and sat in the middle where I had been. With another growl, he pulled me into his lap to straddle him and I grinned through his sexy, possessive kiss. Such a greedy alpha.

As he kissed a fiery trail down my neck, I turned to settle my gaze on Razvan.

"*Now* will you get naked?"

"Oh, I like it so much more when you do it to me, *steluța*," he grinned, leaning back and lacing his hands behind his head.

I leaned my head back, letting my eyes roll as Hunter nibbled the spot between my neck and shoulder. "And you boys call *me* greedy."

Reluctantly, I pulled away from Hunter, who kept his hands lingering on me until the very last moment, and crawled over the armrest to Raz. His gray eyes smoldered as I settled into his lap.

"Hello," I dropped my gaze, suddenly feeling shy under his overpowering intensity.

"Hello, *steluța*," his sexy voice rumbled. He caught my chin and pressed a hot but playful kiss to my mouth. "The most beautiful woman who's ever sat naked in my lap."

He kissed my bashfulness away as I lifted the hem of his shirt, discarding it in some dark corner of the room. My lips and fingers trailed over the dark ink covering him as I worked my way down. Every time I touched him, I seemed to notice a new art piece, a new detail in the greater work of art that was his whole body.

His hands smoothed down my back as my mouth reached his navel, a soft groan escaping as I undid his pants. He lifted his hips for me to slide them down, and those three piercings on the flared edge of his head greeted me like twinkling stars.

I took him in my mouth, already eager to taste him, and loved watching him react. He gripped the armrests, narrowly missing grabbing Hunter's hand, and hissed in a sharp breath. I flicked the underside of his head a few times and watched him squirm before bobbing my head down to take more of him.

"Fucking...Fuck...God..."

"Forget your own name yet, Raz?"

The question came from Connor, somewhere to the right and behind me. I didn't forget him, I would make my way down there, but first—*oh God.*

A large, warm hand cupped my vulva, sending jolts through my clit at the delicious pressure. I yelped in surprise, which came out as a muffled moan with my mouth stuffed and Raz only gripped the armrests harder.

"Can't leave you to do all the work, babe." Kisses poured over my back before a sharp smack on my ass made me squeal.

"Ah, that's right," Raz grinned. "She told us she liked that, Con."

"Revealing my secrets, now? You get another one for that." A smack fell to my opposite cheek so hard, I released Raz's cock to cry out and glare back at him.

"Don't distract her too much. You're ruining my fun," Raz cracked.

"Sorry, dragon." I kissed his pierced head and lapped up the small bead of pre-come that formed. "Your turn to be teased." I slid over to Hunter, shooting Raz a wide, shit-eating grin.

"Oh, so not fair," he whined.

Ignoring him, I raked my fingers up Hunter's thighs and tilted my face up for a kiss. He was almost fully hard already, but I wanted to take my time enjoying him too.

"Melody," Hunter breathed barely above a whisper before kissing me. He said my full name almost like a plea, and his kiss was full of passion and longing.

"Hunter," I answered, a sudden flurry of emotion making my throat thick. "I love you."

He froze. "You do?"

I nodded, suddenly feeling more vulnerable than I ever had with any of them. We both murmured so softly, I couldn't even be sure the other two heard us. It was like the rest of the world just fell away.

A small smile just between us lit up his face, and he kissed me again. He didn't say the words back, but I could feel them. I felt his desire to throw his head back and howl at the moon in victory, to hold on to his mate, to me, with his teeth and fuck her savagely to make his claim.

But we were human now, and I wanted to play with all my mates.

He growled a soft protest as my lips broke away from his, kissing down his lithe, lean body until I settled between his thighs, kneeling on the floor in front of him like he was a king. Much like Razvan, he hissed when I took him in my mouth, teasing his head at first before working my way down the hot shaft.

With my mouth occupied, Connor enjoyed getting what noises he could out of me. His hands on my hips, he stroked his own cock against my entrance, teasing and rubbing with no penetration yet, no matter how much I arched and lifted my hips.

Ever the gentleman, Hunter held my hair out of my face as I stroked him with my fist, my hands meeting my lips on his length in a steady rhythm. My other hand stretched out to my left, determined not to leave my bad boy dragon out of the fun.

"Come closer, Raz," I rasped, catching his eye with my lips against Hunter's silky head. "Let me touch you too."

I didn't need to tell him twice. "Scoot over, wolf. You heard the lady."

The two of them barely fit in the same chair, but they made it work. Raz's dark ink-covered leg pressed against Hunter's pale one, but they didn't touch aside from that. I almost didn't notice their sexy, nervous glances at each other or their breaths growing more ragged now, being in such close proximity to each other. I was too busy feeling like a fucking porn star.

Returning my mouth to Hunter, I gripped the base of Razvan's dick and stroked upward. His whole body jolted as a result, and I knew he was struggling to make good on his promise to not touch Hunter.

"Holy fuck, that's so fucking hot."

I wasn't sure who said it. All three of my men moaned and grunted and cursed, the hottest sounds ever to reach my ears, heightened by all the sensations running through my body. Pulling my mouth away from Hunter, I slid over to Razvan.

"I have died and somehow gone to fucking heaven," he breathed as I sucked him into my mouth again, my hand still stroking Hunter next to him.

Connor chose right then to finally penetrate me,

turning up the heat and frenzied desire in me to a fever pitch. He pulled my hips back hard, impaling me on his length as my head fell back, mouth open like I was trying to keep from drowning.

"Yes, look at you," Razvan stroked down my arms as I fought desperately to hold on through Connor's pounding. "So gorgeous while she's getting fucked. Isn't she, alpha?"

The nickname for Hunter caught me off guard, but Connor reached underneath me to strum my clit just then and every cell in my body chased a pleasure high.

"Mm-hm," the wolf agreed. He wasn't one for much dirty talk, which was fine with me. But as my gaze drifted up to meet his, my pleasure reached a new high when I saw his face.

He couldn't stop staring at Razvan.

Raz, either because he was totally entranced by me or was determined not to make Hunter uncomfortable, looked at me like I was the only other person in the room. He stroked my face, teased my nipples between his fingers, and stroked himself for me while I sucked and licked him as best I could amid Connor fucking me.

Hunter seemed torn in two different directions. He touched me too when I turned to focus on him, but I didn't miss his golden eyes constantly flickering over to the tattooed dragon next to him. All the while, Connor spanked my ass, strummed my clit like an instrument, and marked up my back with his lips and teeth as he surged in and out of me.

Just before my next orgasm threatened to crash over me, when my pleasure crested and I was well and truly drunk on my feelings for these men, I blurted out what had been on my mind since he first walked back into the house.

"Hunter," I moaned. "Just kiss him already."

MELODY

y wolf's eyes widened before he looked at Razvan again, chest rising and falling with his ragged breaths.

The dragon returned his gaze coolly, neither inviting nor pushing him away to do what I asked. He left the choice entirely in Hunter's hands.

Hunter leaned over hesitantly at first, but then the desire swept over his fear and his mouth pressed to Razvan's.

Raz cupped his neck and returned the kiss passionately, sending that split tongue forward to give our wolf some of the same pleasure he gave me, and then I came like a waterfall.

"Jesus fuck," Connor groaned from behind me, pausing his thrusts as my pussy convulsed around him. I only knew it was him because the other two's mouths were occupied.

Watching them was beyond hot, and my orgasm seemed to last forever. But it wasn't just hot, it was intimate and sweet. Raz pulled away for a moment, his forehead against Hunter's, and their eyes locked. Hunter responded by grabbing his tattooed shoulders and pulling him in for another kiss.

My heart wanted to burst with everything I felt for them, and what they seemed to find between each other. If they could give each other any semblance of what they made me feel, I wanted them to have that happiness and passion more than anything.

"Fuck, alpha," Raz groaned, his back arching against the chair.

Hunter's fingers had trailed down his stomach and caressed his tattooed thighs, massaging all around that stiff, iron hard cock that flexed as it begged to be touched. I watched, entranced, as my own hands surrounded Hunter's cock.

"Go ahead. Take care of him, handsome wolf," I grinned, watching him shudder as I returned to stroking him. "I got you. Connor's got me. Take care of our dragon."

He shot me a lopsided grin, still caressing Razvan in an intimate, exploratory way. "You're sure you're okay with this?" He'd given into his feelings now, but still wanted to protect mine.

"Did you just hear me come?" I planted a kiss on his hip. "It's more than okay, my love."

My lips hovered just over the crown of his dick. I wanted to see him stroke Raz, to see the dragon's reaction to his touch.

"Ohhh my fucking God..." Raz fisted Hunter's platinum hair at the base of his skull and pulled him in for another kiss, his hips thrusting in time with Hunter's strokes.

Connor resumed his thrusts inside me, and I licked the salty pre-cum from Hunter's dick. My next orgasm was already building inside me, closer and closer with every one of Hunter's moans, Razvan's pants, and Connor's curses.

To anyone seeing us like this, it would've looked like straight up hedonistic debauchery. Four horny people chasing physical pleasure, but no one but us could see our delicate balance. How much we cared about and supported each other, whether there was sexual attraction or not.

Connor loved and encouraged me getting so turned on by our shifters. Not only that, we both encouraged them to be together for their own happiness. The walls came down today and this moment was special, intimate, and vulnerable.

"You're gonna make me come, wolf," Raz gasped in a ragged pant.

That only spurred Hunter on more, and he grew even stiffer in my mouth as his own orgasm drew near. I took him further down my throat, relishing in the fullness of him while Connor filled me from behind.

"You got me so close, babe," my soldier groaned, his fingers digging into my hips as his thrusts deepened.

Hunter's breath caught in his chest as the first spray of cum coated my tongue. I drank him down greedily just as I heard Razvan growl out his release. For the second time, their pleasure sent me over the edge.

I released Hunter's cock to let out the scream I'd been holding in, my head on his thigh as he pinched my nipples to heighten my pleasure even more. Connor's chest pressed to my back as he released inside me, sweat and sex clinging to both of us.

"Now," I panted, my heart still racing as I planted a kiss on Hunter's knee. "You can go shower."

FRESHLY SHOWERED, fed, and rested from our fun romp in the theater room, I decided to check on Arjun.

I knocked three times softly at the bedroom door and waited. When no answer came, I cracked the door open.

"Arjun?" I called, keeping my voice low in case he was still sleeping, and poked my head in. "It's Melody. How are you feeling?"

The simple futon bed had been freshly made with its sheets and duvet cover tucked under the mattress, but no man or tiger laid in it.

"Arjun?" I crept into the room, looking around at the bare, simple furnishings and taking slow, measured steps.

A deep, rumbling growl sent me spinning with my heart in my throat. The Bengal tiger sat on his haunches, looking at me from the small attached bathroom. His tail swished on the tile floor, inspecting me with a pinned stare, much like a house cat would.

I lowered my eyes to his dinner plate sized paws on the floor, not wanting to challenge this predator with direct eye contact.

Arjun, I'm Melody. A shaman. We've spoken before. Do you remember?

The human man within the tiger didn't answer me, but I felt his presence stronger than before. We seemed to be near each other in the same dark hallway, but without sight to know truly how close.

Would you please shift to human so we can talk properly? I would like to help you. We can take you anywhere you'd like to go. You're free now.

He pulled his lips and ears back and roared, startling me enough to stumble back a few steps. With his massive head low, he brought one paw forward and then the other. Stalking his prey.

I turned and practically flew out of the room as fast as my feet could carry me. Shutting the door behind me, I backed away and waited with bated breath.

Nothing happened.

After a few moments, I heard the distinctive creak of a box spring. The tiger apparently just wanted me out of his room so he could sleep.

Confused, I went in search of Razvan.

Bypassing the theater room, where Hunter and Connor were now watching some sports channel, I spotted the dragon shifter throwing knives at a tree on the edge of the property.

He didn't acknowledge me until I came right up next to him, juggling the silver blades through the air with casual flicks of his wrists.

"Hey," I smiled at him, my heart lifting at the memory of his pleasure from Hunter less than an hour ago.

"*Steluța,*" he greeted me, taking careful aim with his knives before hurtling all four of them at the tree trunk. The sharp blades struck the wood in a perfect diamond pattern.

"I just tried talking to Arjun," I said, walking alongside him as he went to retrieve his knives. "He was in tiger form again and seemed pretty insistent on me staying out of his bedroom."

"He's most likely gone a bit feral," he mused, yanking the handles from the trunk. "It happens to shifters who stay in animal form for too long. They become unbalanced if their human sides don't take form, and they behave more animal than human."

"How can we rebalance him?" I asked, following him back to his throwing spot.

"Just talk to him like he's a person and give him time. I've had to coax him back to human a few times while we were together." He spun the knives on his fingers. "I'll pay him a visit next. A familiar face will help."

"Thank you, dragon." I grabbed his arm and stood on tiptoe to kiss his cheek, only then noticing he barely looked at me the whole time we were out here. "Hey, is something wrong?"

"No." He faced me for the first time, forcing a smile and giving me a quick peck on the lips. "Why?"

"I don't know. You seem a little distant since..." I trailed off, not feeling the need to say, *since you made out with and got stroked off by another man less than an hour ago.*

"I don't mean to be, *steluța*. Just thinking about it, I guess."

"In what way?"

"Nosy girl," he teased, tapping the end of my nose with his index finger. "Not in a bad way, I promise. I enjoyed every second of that and don't regret a thing."

"But it was different than the first time we were together."

"Yes," he breathed. "In a few ways."

"I'll leave you to think," I told him, reluctantly letting

go of his arm. "But if there's anything bothering you, please tell me. You know I can't stand the silent treatment like the other two have done."

He gazed down at me gratefully before giving me a long, deep kiss. "I promise you, I will."

18

RAZVAN

"Arjun," I sighed. "Come on, shift back. You can't be a big damn pussy the rest of your life."

The tiger roared at me, his claws curling out as his massive paws kneaded the duvet cover. Damn cat was already shredding it to ribbons. He'd already scratched up the flooring, too. I hoped the nonprofit center wouldn't charge us for damages.

"I know you feel safer in this form," I told him. "But there's nothing to fear now. You're safe. I promise you that, mate. We just want to help you."

His responding growl was softer as he lowered his head to rest on his paws. Slowly but surely, he was coming around.

"Don't you want to drive a car again?" I asked him. "Walk around town without people running and scream-ing, go to a bar, maybe?"

Like most shifters, I preferred my animal form. The list of things more enjoyable as a human was very short.

For me, driving was on that list. All the basic needs such as food, sex, and comfort could be met without being human.

At least for most animals. I'd never fucked another dragon before.

Arjun licked his paws, then stared at me. A low purr rumbled in his throat. He was hungry again.

"I told you the rules," I said with a shrug. "You eat human food in human form. We don't need any damn rednecks shooting at you in the woods."

He bared his teeth, which slowly began shrinking. The orange fur and black stripes sank back into his hair follicles until it morphed into a light brown tan. He shrank in size, limbs and organs rearranging until a handsome but surly Indian man looked at me from the bed.

"Good enough for you?" he asked in that musical Londoner accent. Mel would be swooning once she heard him actually speak.

"Good man," I answered, straightening up from where I leaned against the wall. "Shall I bring your food up like you're a sick child or will you get dressed and come down yourself?"

"I'll come down," he muttered, pushing himself off the bed to rummage on the floor for his borrowed clothing. "So where is she, the shaman?"

"She's with Connor at the main building. They're running tests and assessing him for new prosthetics."

"Prosthetic what?" he pulled on a pair of Hunter's sweatpants and one of my shirts.

"Legs," I answered. "I forgot, you didn't see him. He's a war veteran. Hard times turned him into a show pony like us." I clapped Arjun on the shoulder as he rounded the bed, already getting a better handle on his human legs. "Let's get some breakfast in you."

"Please tell me you have tea." I allowed him to lean on me as we descended the stairs. "Fuck me, I haven't had a decent cup of tea in ages."

"I'll see what we can do," I chuckled, pleased at hearing his old personality return.

A delicious smell and sizzling sound wafted in from the kitchen. Hunter laid out strips of bacon in a pan, while Roo stood on a footstool, carefully folding over scrambled eggs on the stove next to him. Rinna stood between them, circling around her dad and brother's legs, hoping to catch an extra piece.

"Morning, wolves." I draped an arm over Arjun's shoulders. "This is my friend, Arjun. This is Hunter, Roo, and Rinna."

"Cheers, mate." Arjun bumped fists with Roo and Hunter in greeting. "Might I ask what have you got for tea in this place?"

"Think we have some Earl Grey in the cupboards," Hunter replied, keeping a watchful eye on Roo. We hadn't spoken much since yesterday, and now, without Mel as a sort of buffer between us, it felt like the awkward morning after a one-night stand. I didn't know whether to be affectionate with him in any way or pretend it never happened.

I saw Arjun's teeth clench, but he forced a smile. "That'll do nicely, thanks."

Rinna peered up at Arjun from the floor, lifting her nose to sniff the air delicately. "Are you the big tiger?"

"That I am, love. You've got a good nose on you," Arjun smiled at her.

"Why do you talk funny like Mr. Razvan?"

"Rinna!" Hunter barked a low warning. "That's rude."

But Arjun and I burst into peals of laughter, which only confused the poor girl more. Even Hunter tried to hide a smirk as he focused on cooking the bacon.

"It's alright. No one's given me a good ribbing over my accent in years." Arjun knelt to Rinna's level. "I talk funny because I'm from a place called England. Ever heard of it?"

She shook her head, eyes wide in fascination.

"It's on an island far away from here." He placed his index fingers on the floor. "See, we're here. England is wayyy over here. And there's a big ocean in the middle."

"What ocean is that, Rinna?" Hunter asked in a gentler tone. "You know it."

"The Atlantic Ocean?" she glanced up at her father hesitantly.

"Very good!" He turned off the stove and smoothed a hand over her dark hair before bending down to kiss her head. "Now sit at the table. Food's ready."

"Now Mr. Razvan talks funny," Arjun continued, slowly easing himself into a seat at the table. "'Cause he's a damned Eastern European who didn't even speak a lick of English until a few years ago."

"Yeah, what else do you speak, you damned imperialist?" I shot back with a slug to his arm.

"Hindi," he retorted. "And Bengali. And Urdu. And *proper* English. All since birth, mind you."

"Whatever," I muttered, heaping eggs and bacon on two large plates while Hunter portioned out smaller plates for the kids. "Thanks for breakfast, Hunter."

"Of course." He touched my waist, and then I felt the unmistakable warmth and softness of his lips on my neck. His mouth connected right behind my ear, ironically right where I had a black lipstick mark tattooed. My heart crashed against my ribs while my whole body froze, and then the sensation was gone.

Unfreezing from my stupor, I turned around. The scene at the table carried on like no one noticed. Roo and Rinna excitedly asked Arjun to say words in his other native languages while Hunter attempted to settle them down to eat. Arjun indulged them and even traced Sanskrit words on the table with his fingers. The guy was truly brilliant, even if he was an English prick sometimes.

"Thanks, love." He made a kissing noise at me as I set his plate in front of him, then grinned a broad, pearly smile. "Where's my tea, then?"

"I think I liked you better as a cat," I muttered, returning to the cupboards to rummage for the Earl Grey.

"Oh, don't lie. You missed my cheeky self."

I kept my grin to myself as I prepared a tea bag in a cup of hot water. Truthfully, I did miss the big striped bastard. Even in the darkest, most bleak of times during our captivity, his cheeky attitude kept me going. Even now, after nearly seeing his own end, he could smile at the kids and give me a well-deserved ribbing.

"So we are still in the States, I take it?" he asked around a mouthful of eggs.

"Yes, Georgia," Hunter informed him.

"Ah, still in redneck central, I see."

We filled him in on our journey since meeting Mel and coming to this place. He listened with rapt attention, his blue-green eyes shifting from Hunter to me as we spoke.

"Hold on a moment," Arjun raised a hand after listening to what we knew of Mel's shaman abilities. "How old is she?"

"Eighteen," Hunter answered. "As of a month or so ago."

Arjun's eyes widened, his hand moving to his jaw that dropped open. "That is… unheard of. A shaman so young, tapping into her power already. Communicating with her mind across distances?" He shook his head. "I've known a few in my life and have never seen that."

"What's your experience been with shamans?" Hunter asked.

"My mother married one," Arjun explained. "He wasn't my sire, obviously, but he raised me and my siblings. Not a lot of great places for tigers to be out and about in London, you see, so he protected us. He could cast illusions so human eyes wouldn't notice us. A few years before I got captured, he was training a young lady shaman. I got to sit in on some of their lessons. Fascinating stuff."

His jaw clenched as he took a sip of tea. I knew his mother died when he was younger, but he never elaborated when it happened. Something told me he wasn't too happy about his stepfather taking a young female shaman under his wing, despite learning what they were capable of.

"So Mel is advanced for her age?" I asked, turning the subject back to her.

"Highly." He nodded. "She definitely needs training, though. The way she comes through my head is quite messy and jumbled. Sometimes I couldn't tell if she was another tiger shifter nearby. Her illusion powers are strong but she needs better control of them."

"I thought she was another dragon at one point too," I added.

"Connor told me, I think when she was first tapping into you, Arjun," Hunter chuckled, "that he nearly pissed himself because he heard a growl and swore there was a massive animal in bed with him."

"Can we go outside, Dad?" Roo asked, looking up proudly from his empty plate.

"Yes, you may."

"Can we shift?" Rinna slid out of her chair.

"Only if you stay behind the house," Hunter told her sternly. "I mean it. Do not let any humans see you."

"Okay, Dad!" They tore off running toward the back-yard, Roo already letting out high-pitched puppy howls.

"Adorable pups, mate," Arjun beamed, glancing back at them. "You've done good."

"Thank you. They're a handful, but I try," Hunter sighed, leaning back and lacing his hands behind his head. "It's hard without a pack, but they've taken really well to our group of misfits here."

"So, now that it's only adults at the table," Arjun cleared his throat. "Perhaps you can tell me. Are all of you with her?"

"Yes, we are," I answered quickly. "It's not the most traditional situation, but it seems to be working for us."

"I see. I was just wondering because it's not unusual for shamans to form polyamorous relationships with all the shifters they keep close."

"The shaman woman we met at the carnival alluded to that," Hunter smirked. "Most of them are female and they tend to form harems."

"Well, aren't you blokes lucky," Arjun cheeked behind another sip of tea.

"We are," I agreed with no humor in my voice. "She saved Hunter and his kids. She talked Connor into getting help for his many issues. And she saved *your* ass. You're just as lucky as we are, Arjun."

"And I'm grateful," he replied, leveling his gaze to mine. "I'm sure she's a lovely woman and I look forward to speaking with her properly. But there's no way I'm standing in line behind other blokes competing for a woman's affection."

"That's not really how it is, but fair enough," Hunter remarked with a casual shrug.

Satisfied, Arjun drained his mug of tea and sat back. "Thanks for breakfast, Hunter. That was delicious. I feel my human taste buds coming back already."

"Welcome back to the world of two legs and dulled senses." Hunter laughed as he stood to clear plates from the table. "Raz, when are Mel and Connor supposed to come back?"

"Some time in the afternoon, depending on how long his physical therapy goes," I muttered, rising to help him with dishes. I avoided Mel again this morning, which I hated doing. I could only hope this ache would pass with time, or until she said the words to make it go away instantly, but I didn't hold out much hope for that.

Hunter noticed the lack of enthusiasm in my reply and lifted an eyebrow in question as I stacked plates next to the sink.

"I'm off for a catnap," Arjun said with a yawn and stretch above his head. "Catch up with you blokes later."

Hunter and I watched him go up the stairs, most of the wobbliness gone from his legs as he held the railing. He'd be at full human strength in no time.

"Something on your mind?" the wolf asked me once we

were alone. His hands brushed against mine as he took dishes from me to soak in the sink.

"When is there not?" I laughed nervously, my heart returning to its violent assault on my sternum. Where could I even begin? I wanted to tell him, but where did I stand with this man?

"Are you bothered because of yesterday?" he asked, his voice low and his golden eyes fixated on the dishes in the sink.

I looked at him, watching his shoulders flex as his hands moved. "Because of you and me? No." My hand slid to the small of his back, resting in the curve just above his ass. "How could I be?" I brought my lips to his shoulder to emphasize my point. "Have you done that to another man before?"

He gave a small shake of his head as a faint blush rose in his pale cheeks. I smiled against his shoulder, breathing in his earthy scent as my arm wrapped around to skim my fingertips across his abs.

"Well, you fooled me, alpha."

"Done it to myself plenty of times, though," he laughed, his eyes meeting mine shyly. "Have you?"

"Yeah. It's been so long, though. I usually prefer women but," I stepped in closer to feel the heat of his side against my torso, "sometimes there's a rare exception."

He lifted his hands from the soapy water and wiped them on a towel before wrapping his fingers around mine and turned to face me.

"So something else is bothering you?"

I sighed. The wolf was so perceptive, he wouldn't even allow me a distraction.

"I heard what Mel said to you in the heat of the moment."

"That she loves me?" His brow furrowed with concern as his fingers squeezed around mine.

"Yeah," I admitted. "That in itself doesn't bother me, but... she loves *you*. She loves *Connor*. I'm just wondering where I fit in. If I fit in at all."

"Raz." Hunter brought his hands together around the back of my neck, lowering his forehead to mine. With a hitched breath, I brought my hands to his forearms, grateful for him being there while I didn't want to look like a whiny bitch in front of Mel.

"I thought I'd be okay with just being her toy," I admitted. "The tattooed bad boy she entertained herself with while she had more meaningful relationships with others. But...I can't."

"Raz," Hunter breathed again, his lips inches from mine. "She doesn't see you that way. She never has. She's absolutely smitten with you. Just give her time. I'm positive she is in love with you, or will be soon."

"I dunno, man. I'm starting to feel like a third wheel and it honestly fucking hurts." I released his forearms, moving to step away from him. "I don't want to get in the way of—"

He cut me off with a growl and a hard kiss, pulling my body flush against his. Fire surged through me, my dragon roaring for more from this wolf. I bit down hard on his lip and Hunter just returned it, his teeth feeling pointier than normal. This wasn't anything like kissing a woman, this was two alpha animals warring for dominance.

Hunter grabbed my wrists and turned both of our bodies to slam my back against the wall with a loud crack. It would've knocked any mere human unconscious, but he felt my dragon fighting for release. I barely registered my head bumping against the wall, only letting out a reptilian snarl from the impact. Hunter's hot erection pressing against mine held all of my attention. That and his sharp canine teeth only inches from my face.

"You're *not* a third wheel. I don't ever want you to say or think that," he growled, his words slightly muffled by the shift in his jaws. "We're individuals, Raz. Her feelings are going to develop differently for all of us. Be patient and believe that. You can't force her feelings, so don't mope and feel sorry for yourself, dragon."

"Fine," I groaned. "You're right. I just need to get my head out of my ass."

Hunter's teeth shrank back to human size and his grip loosened as he shot me a wily smirk. "You want to know something?"

"Hm?" I tried to keep my attention focused on his face, not his tall, lean body pinning me to the wall.

"I probably wouldn't have kissed you or touched you at all if she hadn't told me she loved me."

"Oh?" I lifted a brow. "What's one got to do with the other?"

"She knew about me feeling attracted to you." His eyes flickered down. "And she still loves me. Just knowing she accepted me feeling this way and loving me despite it? That was the final push I needed to act on it. To know for sure that this was okay."

"You got one thing wrong, wolf," I laughed dryly, pushing away from the wall to tease the length of his neck with my tongue.

"What's that?" he groaned, hooking his fingers in my belt loops and pulling me against him.

"Did you see how hard she came?" I grazed my teeth along his earlobe, relishing in the hot shudder that followed. "She loves you *because* of who you are, not in spite of it."

19

HUNTER

A mixture of scents filled my nose as I ran—rabbit, fox, pheasant. But this wasn't a hunt, nor a run to escape from anything I was feeling. This was a run of exhilaration and joy with two of my favorite people.

Roo and Rinna followed at my heels. I kept my pace slow enough for them to stay close, but just enough to push them. They needed the challenge to become strong wolves.

I smelled water a few hundred feet away and picked up the pace. Just a bit farther until we reached our spot to rest before heading back home.

Home. I never thought that word would consist of two humans and two other shifters of a different species. Razvan, Mel, Connor—they'd all been abandoned by their own kind. I began to see how lucky I was to grow up with my pack, that my two pups knew other wolves in their young lives. But as they grew older, those memories would only grow more distant.

I worried for them, as much as I loved how the others

took to them. If our family of misfits stayed together, my pups would grow up safe, happy, and cared for. Ultimately, that was all I really wanted. What worried me was when they'd want mates of their own. Would any pack accept them?

We reached the stream, slowing our run to a canter. The pups panted behind me as I lowered my black nose to the water, sniffing before taking a drink. They slurped at the trickling water greedily, thankfully knowing better than to drink it in human form. When we took our fill, I sat on my haunches and shifted back to human.

Sometimes I liked feeling the effects of a good run better in a human body than a wolf. My two animals just didn't feel adrenaline and excitement the same way. Right then, I was running on the high of being with Razvan in the kitchen.

The recollection brought a smirk to my mouth and a fluttering in my chest. My run felt fast and light with relief. He returned what I felt and showed me I didn't have to carry shame or guilt like a heavy burden.

And Mel... she loved me.

I loved her back. God knew I did. But the pack mentality held me in its strong jaws. I couldn't just get over it, like Connor said. Pack law dictated wolf shifters take mates of the same species. No humans and definitely no dragons.

Wolf packs weren't perfect, of course. Many of them were run by grizzled old alphas stuck in backward ways of thinking. But we had community when so many shifters had to go through life alone. We banded together and protected our own whenever confronted by humans. As a rebellious adolescent wolf, I had my issues with how much the pack dictated my personal life. But now, as an adult and father, I yearned for my pups to have that same kind of community to protect them.

Roo shifted to human after a few moments of resting on the bank of the stream. "Dad, why were you and Mr. Razvan hugging like that in the kitchen?"

I bit the inside of my cheek to hold back my laugh. He was almost seven now and so observant. Nothing got past my boy. I knew I'd have to tell them about this, eventually.

"Sometimes two males or two females like each other in the same way as a male and female do," I told him.

"Oh, like an omega."

"Kind of," I said, smoothing out his golden white hair. "Only Mr. Razvan would never be at the bottom of the pack. He's very strong."

"Yeah," my son agreed, quietly taking in this information as he looked at me. "So you like both? Since you kiss Miss Mel a lot too."

"I guess I do," I said. "Raz is the first male I like in that way, and I tried to ignore it at first."

"Why?" he seemed genuinely surprised and my heart tugged painfully in my chest.

Summer was almost over and he'd need to start school soon. I hoped he would never witness the tormenting that I saw in human schools. Omegas were a long-accepted part of wolf society. They lived at the bottom of the pack hierarchy and sometimes were sexual bottoms for other male wolves if there were no available females around. But humans were especially cruel to their own people who they speculated were gay.

"Humans don't really have omegas in their society," I explained. "Sometimes men who like other men are treated really badly for no reason. Women too. A lot of them hide it. It's not right, but it's what they have to do sometimes in order to survive."

"Humans are dumb," Roo muttered, drawing in the muddy stream bank with an index finger. "Not Mel or Mr. Connor, though."

"You're right about that." I ruffled his hair again and leaned back on my elbows to just listen to the stream. Roo shifted back to wolf to wrestle with Rinna. Their playful snarls and yelps brought a smile to my face and a sense of peace over me.

I didn't know entirely how I felt about Raz and tried to be okay with that. It was more than just physical, although those feelings didn't run as deep as they did for Mel. Not yet anyway. And I certainly liked each of them for different reasons, as I imagined she liked all of us.

I loved her sweetness, how soft she was, how she just melted under my touch. I liked his strength, that I could be rougher with him. Every little fight for dominance we had made me hard.

A good alpha never got comfortable. He was always challenged, always proving his worth of holding his position. Raz spoke to that primal part of me. As long as we had Mel and the kids to protect, he'd never let me get lazy.

But he had a softness about him too. I saw it whenever he looked at Mel, and for a moment in the kitchen when he admitted to feeling like a third wheel.

I liked that he opened up to me. He could come to me when he wasn't sure about talking to Mel, and I hoped it made him feel better. We didn't go further in the kitchen other than the hot kiss and a little slamming against the wall. Neither of us felt right about doing more without

Mel around, and I was glad we were on the same page about that.

A shift in the air brought a scent to my nose that made me freeze and listen.

That scent was familiar, one I hadn't smelled in what felt like ages.

No, how could it be...

And just as quickly, it was gone.

I swiveled my head, trying to pick it up again, but all I caught were faint whiffs. The spark of hope in my chest dissipated. An old scent then, probably from months ago. The breeze just happened to carry it right under my nose.

I laid out on my back, stretching my abs and spine to get ready for the run back.

Back home, where my family was safe, and I was loved for being me.

20

MELODY

I followed after Connor in a huff. Every day he seemed faster in that damned wheelchair, despite being so averse to it at first.

"Slow down, Con." I broke into a jog, my shoes crunching on the gravel driveway leading up to our house.

I still couldn't believe those words. Our house.

"Catch up to me, babe," he laughed, pulling himself up the steps of the porch with the pure brute strength of his arms. The house came equipped with a wheelchair ramp on the left side of the wraparound porch, but of course, he refused to use it.

"Where's my bacon, Hunter?" he yelled as he wheeled inside, his voice echoing off the slanted ceiling.

"Get your own. I'm busy!" came the reply.

"Busy doing wha—Oh, I see how it is!"

"Jesus, why do y'all gotta be so loud when we have a guest resting?" I grumbled, following the cacophony into the theater room.

Someone swapped two of the armchairs with the

loveseat from the reading area. Stretched out on the loveseat, watching *Jeopardy!*, was Hunter. His long legs dangled over the edge, entwined with Razvan's, who laid on top of him with his head on the wolf's chest.

"Oh my gosh, you guys are so cute," I gushed. They looked so cozy and comfortable together. A mixture of relief and a fresh burst of love for both of them made my heart lift. I was so happy to see they got over any shame or uncertainty and were comfortable enough to be openly affectionate with each other.

"Connor, where's your phone? I want to take a picture of them."

"This cuddle pile is open if you'd like to join us," Hunter grinned lazily.

"We need a bigger couch," Raz mumbled, sighing contently.

Before I could answer, heavy, lumbering steps came down the stairs, and I found myself face-to-face with a tiger.

"Hello, Arjun," I said, trying to keep my voice steady. "Have you rested well?"

Something about him made me more afraid than I ever felt with Hunter or Raz. Maybe because I saw him kill a man through his own eyes, or how he came at me when I was in his bedroom the other day. Or maybe it was just the raw, predatory power that flowed through him with every feline step.

The tiger pounced, and a scream caught in my throat.

He landed right on top of Raz and Hunter, then proceeded to just sit on them.

"Jesus fuck! Get off you bastard, you're fucking heavy!"

Arjun parted his jaws in a wide yawn and ignored the

thrashing shifters underneath him, choosing to knead his massive paws on Razvan's back instead.

"Ow! Cut that out, you're not a fucking house cat!"

The tiger huffed out a breath before his form shrank down, shifting to human.

"No fun, the lot of you," he sighed disappointedly, propping his elbow on the edge of the loveseat.

"Um," I shielded my eyes, heat rising in my cheeks. "Did you forget about clothes?"

"I most certainly did not," he replied with amusement. "I heard an open invitation to a cuddle pile, which my tiger just happens to love."

"You weren't invited," Raz joked, slugging him on the arm. "Girls only."

Arjun lifted a well-defined eyebrow. "Right. Girls only invited to your cuddle party with another man. That makes perfect sense."

"Can you please put something on?" Ironically, the one man I didn't sleep with seemed to be the most comfortable sitting around nude while the rest of us were fully clothed like normal people. And damn it, why did he have to have an accent and be so good-looking too?

"My apologies. I've been a bit out of touch with my humanity as of late." The snark in his voice indicated it was far from a sincere apology, but I heard his bare foot-steps pad back up the stairs again.

"He takes some getting used to," Raz chuckled. "He's English, you see."

"Really? I hadn't noticed," I stammered, flustered. I wanted to fan my face, but didn't want to give the guys another excuse to tease me.

"He's a good guy, though. And brilliant. Probably one of the few shifters left who knows a lot about shamans."

"Well then, let's hope we can get along," I murmured. Already I wasn't sure if Arjun and I would be able to have a normal conversation, let alone any kind of friendship. He seemed entirely too arrogant and rubbed me the wrong way.

Moments later, he came back down the stairs wearing a borrowed pair of sweatpants and dark green t-shirt that made his eyes pop. They looked like the bluish-green hue of a tropical ocean.

"Does this satisfy Her Majesty's requirements?" he asked, smirking as he held his hands out to his sides.

"Yes, thanks." I ignored his sarcastic remark, tearing my gaze from his as I ran my fingers through my hair. "Anyway, back to your cuddling and *Jeopardy!*-watching. Con and I are hungry so I'll see about some dinner."

"Oh, and now she's refusing the 'girl's only' cuddle invitation! I gotta say, guys," Arjun shook his head as he reclined in one of the armchairs, "I don't know about this shaman."

Connor, who had been in the room but observing silently the whole time, chuckled as he wheeled after me into the kitchen.

"Don't tell me you think he's actually funny," I whispered, opening the refrigerator with a violent pull.

"He kind of is, but I'm not laughing at that." He braked his chair abruptly. "I'm laughing at you."

"What the hell for?"

"'Cause you really are a greedy girl." His lips pulled back into a wide grin. "You want him."

"I do not!"

"You definitely do. If you didn't, you wouldn't care if he was naked."

"Yes, I would have! Connor, there are children in this house!"

"Shifter children," he pointed out. "Who would probably never be wearing clothes if they didn't have to integrate into human society."

"Well, whatever. He clearly doesn't like me." I pulled things out of the fridge at random and set them on the counter.

"He does, though. That's why he's being a pain in your ass. Or *arse*, I should say," he giggled.

"Doesn't seem very mature."

"He's a Brit, babe. Their sense of humor is different. They take the piss out of each other all the time."

"I don't even know what that means."

"They just mess with each other. It's how they show friendliness. If he didn't like you, he'd completely ignore your existence."

"I think I'd prefer that, honestly."

Connor placed his hands on the countertop and pulled himself up to sit on it, twisting around to face me.

"Do you trust my judgement of people, babe?" He pulled out a knife and cutting board, proceeding to prep what I'd taken out of the fridge.

"Of course I do. Except," I giggled, "for when you called that physical therapist an asshole today."

"He *was* being an asshole."

"He was doing his job! He had to figure out which nerves your pain was coming from."

"Yeah, you think he needed to prod me fifty fucking times to figure it out?"

We bantered back and forth as our ingredients came together as BLTs. I made extras for the other guys, including Arjun, while Connor and I just ate at the counter. It was strangely nostalgic, eating and talking like this, like when we first met and it was just me and him in his trailer. Not that I wanted to go back to how things were before the other guys, but I realized these little moments were just ours, and ours alone.

"Come here," he said gruffly, pulling me into a bacon-tomatoey kiss.

"Aren't you happy for Hunter and Raz?" I whispered, my grin threatening to split my face. I couldn't get over seeing them cuddling on the couch. It was downright the most adorable thing I'd ever seen.

"I am," he smirked back. "So you love Hunter, huh?"

"Yes," I admitted. "Does that—"

"Bother me? No, of course not." He kissed me again. "What about Raz?"

"I... I dunno yet." I chewed my lip, lowering my gaze. "I have the biggest crush on him, obviously."

"Almost as big as your crush on Arjun," he teased.

"Shut up," I smacked his chest. "I mean, I like everything about him. He's so open and caring with me. I trust him and I know he takes that very seriously. Just a touch or look from him makes me all fluttery."

"But?" Connor prompted.

"But I do feel a little guarded with him," I admitted. "Because he did hurt me intentionally. Not only that, he hurt another girl intentionally. That first kiss was no accident, and he didn't regret it. I've forgiven him and I trust it not to happen again. It's just that you or Hunter would've never done that in the first place, you know?"

"Hunter and I have hurt you in our own ways," he pointed out. "I'll tell you a secret. We're knuckleheads. All men are."

"Don't I know it," I snorted, wrapping a hand around his neck. "But you're *my* knuckleheads."

"Damn right." He helped himself to firm handfuls of my ass. "We're not perfect, and we're definitely not angels. But we all love you and we're trying our best."

"And I love you." I pressed a kiss to his luscious mouth. "Raz too, I'm sure. I just need to feel right before I say it."

"And that's fine. He's trying his best to be patient and understanding, but it wounded him a little that you told Hunter and not him."

"Shit." I stiffened in his arms, suddenly feeling like the world's biggest asshole. "He told you that?"

"No, but I can just tell. I think that's why he's cozying up to Hunter right now."

"I'm so fucking stupid." I dropped my forehead into my hands. "I just blurted it out. I should have told Hunter in a more private moment. I didn't even think about Raz."

"It's okay, babe. Like I said, he understands, and I think Hunter explained it to him, too. The last thing any of us want to do is force your feelings a certain way." He lifted my chin and those forest green eyes filled my world. "There's three of us and one of you. We all love you and want your love in return, but we're trying not to make a competition about it. It's hard, babe. I get it."

"You're the best, you know that?" I sighed. "It's like you're the elected representative of our whole group. You understand all of us and know how to mediate everything."

"I don't know how my curmudgeonly ass got that job, but I'll take it."

I giggled, nuzzling him for more kisses, which he gave in spades. "I love you so much."

"I love you more," he replied gruffly, trapping me between his muscular thighs. "Damn, I can't wait to get some new legs so I can fuck you against the wall again."

"So romantic." I rolled my eyes. "How long did Dr. Selow say, a week?"

"Too fucking long," he groaned. "But yes, they'll get the first prototypes in a week. I'll try them out but it could be months of fine tuning and calibrating before I get a long term set."

"That's a good thing, though," I said. "Better to make sure they're perfect for you instead of hurting you after a couple years like the other ones."

"Right. And I'll need your help in doing some very thorough testing over those months."

"Oh yeah, like what?"

"They need to pass the fucking you against the wall tests."

"Jesus, Connor..."

21

ARJUN

The shaman was like nothing I expected. She was so young to be so in touch with her abilities already, which was impressive enough. Even Miriam, the girl my stepfather Lhozen had trained, had been in her late twenties when she started having visions.

For being so young, though, Melody sure did seem to have a stick up her arse.

All the guys' tongue wagging and puppy dog eyes were a bit much as well. Even the non-shifter human with no feet looked at her like the sun rose and set from a twirl of her fingers.

Even so, she was the reason I was still alive, the reason I hadn't offed myself earlier despite the utter hopelessness of the situation. The least I could do was help her grasp her shaman abilities.

She and the human man, Connor, spent a while in the kitchen while Raz, Hunter and I resumed watching TV. I squirmed uncomfortably in the chair, in my soft human skin. My tiger itched to come out. He didn't understand why I needed to be a weak, two-legged human. Truthfully, I was having a hard time remembering myself.

Driving is easier as a human, like Raz said, I reminded myself. Drinking tea is also much easier without a gargantuan mouth and tongue.

Tea sounded excellent right then, so I excused myself from watching the too-bright screen and headed into the kitchen. My balance was coming back, although a tail and four legs were much easier. I barely had to lean against the wall when I rounded the corner.

Melody jumped and stared at me wide-eyed, like she'd been caught doing something nefarious. Connor was out of his wheelchair and sitting on the counter, with Melody standing between his thighs and his hands inside her shirt.

"Now, don't stop on my account," I grinned. "Just passing through for some tea."

"I got you, bro." Connor turned and opened the cabinet behind him to hand me the box of Earl Grey. Melody only blushed, her eyes darting away from me.

I itched to make a joke about where his hands had been, but bit my tongue. Melody didn't seem to need any more sticks up her bum from me, at least not right then.

"Cheers, mate." I accepted the box from him and flicked on the electric kettle for my water.

Melody cleared her throat. "There are BLT sandwiches in the fridge if you're hungry. We made a bunch for everyone."

"Lovely. Don't mind if I do." I helped myself to one as my water heated up. My tiger didn't have a taste for tomato or bread, but these simple human staples sent my taste buds into overdrive. Maybe I could get used to staying in human form yet.

"What kind of food do you like?" the young shaman asked. "We can get some more variety tomorrow."

"Assuming you mean human food," I smirked, "I'm not terribly picky. Although I'd be right chuffed to have a good lamb curry again."

"Oh, okay." She sounded unsure and looked a bit sheepish. "I don't think I've ever eaten curry before."

"Never had curry? Have you lived under a fucking rock, woman?"

"No." Her eyes fluttered away as she stepped away from Connor. "In a trailer." Abruptly, she turned and walked out of the kitchen, leaving me and her man to look at each other awkwardly.

"I meant no offense," I said sheepishly. "My mouth goes before I think sometimes."

"She's sensitive about where she's from," he replied in an even tone, indicating he wasn't angry with me. "Traveling across state lines and joining the carnival is the most culture shock she's ever experienced."

"We haven't exactly gone off on the right foot, have we?" I ran a hand through my hair, feeling like a right arsehole. "She must think I'm one hell of a prick."

He lifted one shoulder in a shrug to say that I wasn't wrong.

"I wouldn't go that far, but she is a bit sensitive and thinks you don't like her."

"Well, shit." I switched off the electric kettle a bit more aggressively than necessary as it started to steam. "I don't dislike her, but I don't even know the girl. Yeah, she saved my life but I'm not going to go all starry-eyed for her like you lot."

"She's not expecting you to be like that. She just," he

paused for a moment, rubbing his jaw in thought, "she's not used to people making fun of her as a way of being friendly. She grew up being teased and belittled with malicious intent, so she takes that stuff personally."

"Shit," I muttered again, steeping my tea bag. "So I really am a prick."

"Maybe a little," he laughed, then gave me a good-natured slap on the shoulder. "We all are, though. That's what I was just telling her."

"With your hands on her tits, yeah? A likely story."

"We've all learned to multitask here," he chuckled, lowering himself off the counter and back into his chair with surprising control and strength. He never once touched the floor.

"Apparently." I stirred a sugar cube into my tea. "Pardon me for asking, but do you "multitask" with Hunter and Raz as well?"

"Nah, I'm straight as an arrow. I always had an inkling those two weren't, though, despite how they felt for Mel. Not that there were any tells, really. It was just a strong instinct I had."

"Really?" I took a sip of tea, carefully studying this American patriot without a drop of shifter blood in him. "Are you a shaman as well?"

"Me? Hell no," he laughed. "I just know how to observe people. The Marines taught me to be perceptive. When I lost my legs, it was astounding how differently people treated me. I learned how to see through facades and figure out people's genuine motivations."

"And yet this young shaman woman fell in love with you," I said. "Pardon me for being blunt. It's just that shamans often write off other humans after being around shifters for so long."

"You don't have to apologize for anything," he said, raising a hand. "I appreciate bluntness and guarantee you, there's nothing special about me. If Mel leaves me in the dust to ride off into the sunset with you shifters, I'll accept that decision. In our time together, she's made me a better man. Dare I say, a happy one. And that's more than I ever dreamed of for myself."

"Well, I'll be damned." I leaned against the counter, teacup in hand. "She's really had an effect on all of you, hasn't she?"

"She and them, if I'm being honest," he nodded toward the theater room where Hunter and Raz were undoubtedly still cupcaking. "They're good dudes. Some of the best I've ever known. We've all had shit happen to us and deserve real, genuine happiness. If that means sharing one amazing woman, it's a no brainer. She inspires all of us to be better, and we take care of her when someone's being a prick," he chuckled. "Because someone always is."

❧ 22 ❧

MELODY

"Who wants to come with me to apply for a job?" I asked at breakfast the next morning.

Six pairs of eyes stared back at me as I announced the question.

"A job where?" Roo asked me, pieces of scrambled eggs stuck to his lip.

"There's a carnival not far from here," I told him, wiping his mouth with a napkin. "In a bigger city. I can try to be a ringmistress there again."

"I want to go with you!" Rinna announced.

"No," Hunter and I both said in unison, our eyes meeting across the table.

"You don't need to work, sweetie," I said. "Not until you're older. Right now your job is to become a big, strong wolf."

"But I want to go with you!"

"Hey, shush. Inside voice," Hunter chastised her.

"I'll go with you, *steluța*," Raz offered. "I've been

itching to breathe a little fire and play with my blades again."

"Thank you, dragon." I rubbed his calf with my foot under the table. Secretly, I hoped he'd be the one to volunteer. His theatrical skills would be the most likely to land us a job. Not to mention I wanted some more alone time with him.

"Tell me you're bloody joking," Arjun interjected. It took everything in me not to fling food at him.

"I'm not," Raz answered simply.

The Englishman's blue-green eyes bounced between Raz and I incredulously.

"You're seriously hoping to get a job at *another* carnival? Might I remind you, shaman, you've got three, no, five shifters here, including the little ones, who've escaped from such places. And you want to go back to another one to earn money?"

"My best skills are as a ringmistress," I answered as coolly as I could muster. "I have no other job experience and we can't stay here forever. Plus, getting inside will get me close to more shifters who need help."

"You're bloody eighteen years old! Go to uni. Get a job at McDonald's or whatever kids your age do. You're not helping shifters when you're putting money directly into these people's pockets. Even if you rescue one, the cash flowing from their new ringmistress will just replace that one with another."

"Great, Arjun. Thanks for letting me know I never should have helped you," I said, rising from the table.

"*Steluța—*"

But I was already gone, stomping through the house and fuming. Who fucking asked him for his opinion? And if he thought it was such a terrible idea, why didn't he just let those other humans kill him?

I found myself in the backyard, but not even the beautiful morning light through the trees or the fresh pine smell in the air could pull me out of my funk. Thanks to that tiger asshole, my day was thoroughly ruined.

In that moment, I wished I could turn into a wolf and just race through the woods like Hunter. I could clear my head, feel the cool earth underneath my paws, and hear nothing but the wind in my ears.

I closed my eyes and pictured it like I had in my dreams. Foliage rushed past me, all kinds of smells and sounds filled my senses but none of it was overwhelming. To my canine brain, it made sense. The rabbit's scent trail triggered my instinct to give chase. I was light and silent on my four red paws.

Wait, red?

A sudden hand on my shoulder pulled me back to human awareness.

"You look cute with those ears. What are you seeing through, a fox?" Razvan kissed my cheek and settled on the porch next to me.

"Um, I think so?" I reached up and felt fluffy triangular ears on top of my head before they disappeared. "I don't know how that happened. I was thinking of running through the woods like a wolf."

"Hm. Too bad the person who can explain that to you was a dick at breakfast."

"No shit," I grumbled. "I know he's your friend, but I think I'm better off learning this shaman stuff on my own. I can't seem to have one single interaction with him and not feel like shit."

"I'm not here to convince you otherwise." His fingers drifted across my back. "That was uncalled for, and I told him off just now. Even if he is my friend, I don't like to see you upset."

I leaned my head on his shoulder, grateful that he was just here for me and not to defend Arjun. After what Connor said last night, I was open to giving the tiger shifter another chance and try not to take his jabs personally. But this morning seemed to erase all possibilities of that.

Razvan pressed his lips to my temple. "Want a lesson in throwing knives? It's a good way to let off some steam without actually stabbing anyone."

"Sure. Can I pretend the tree is Arjun's face?"

"Arjun's, mine, your mother's. Whoever you want."

I couldn't help but laugh as he pulled me to my feet. The thought of my mother's bloated, drunk face in a tree trunk was strangely cathartic. With just a few words, my dragon shifter already made me feel better. I shook off the thought that followed, which was Jeanie still hadn't called Connor's phone.

That was just another reason I needed a job. She and my other siblings needed me.

Fuck whatever Arjun thought.

I SUCKED AT THROWING KNIVES. My first dozen or so throws went way wide of my target, which was already the widest tree in our backyard. When they did hit the trunk, they clattered uselessly to the ground with no real strength behind them.

Raz was a patient teacher, however. He reminded me of when Connor first taught me the routine to act with him onstage. The tattooed dragon spoke gently as he gave me instructions and made every excuse to touch me as he corrected mistakes in my form.

His hands tightened on mine around the handles to adjust my grip, then slid down the outsides of my thighs to adjust my feet. I didn't know how I was able to concentrate at all with his fingertips grazing over me and his breath on my ear, but eventually I sank all four knives into that trunk.

"Great job, *steluţa*," he praised me with a smile as we went to retrieve them. "You're a fast learner."

"Thanks! You're a good teacher." He really was, and far more skilled than that old pervert, Syko. Really, the two weren't even comparable. I only thought Syko had skill because I'd never truly seen a gifted knife thrower before. Thank God he never did end up stabbing me.

Upon closer inspection, my knives still went wide of the crudely drawn target he made on the trunk. Two went high and the other two went low, but hey, they all landed!

I meant to pull the knives out, but decided I had a better idea.

Turning around and leaning my back against the trunk, I grabbed Raz's shirt in my fist and pulled him in with a naughty grin.

His mouth crashed to mine with a surprised grunt, then I felt his smile against my lips as he pressed flush against me, pinning me between himself and the tree.

I remembered what Connor said and kissed him harder. Maybe I wasn't ready to say the words yet, but I wanted him to know my feelings went deep and true. I didn't feel more for Connor or Hunter, I just loved them differently. These men held three equal-sized pieces of my heart, but they all occupied different chambers.

The heart has four chambers.

I pushed the random anatomy fact out of my head as my arms slid around Raz's neck, scratching the short, dark hair covering his scalp.

"Mm, I should teach you things more often," he murmured.

"I agree," I whispered, wanting to sink into this private moment between us and feel it wrap around me like a blanket. We had some alone time together while driving and back in Crying Falls, but not like this.

"You really are a fantastic teacher, you know?" I lifted my gaze to his steel-colored eyes. "And a good listener. You're just... really good to me and I appreciate you. I want you to know that."

He blinked as if dumbfounded. I wondered if anyone told him anything like that before, let alone that they loved him. Those three words suddenly found themselves on the tip of my tongue, but he silenced me with another kiss before they could escape.

"I'm a bit at a loss for words," he chuckled, lowering his forehead to mine and running his thumb across my cheekbone. "But I'm touched. Thank you."

"I knew there was a total sweetheart underneath all this ink," I teased him, wanting to lighten the mood.

"Ah, don't tell anyone. I have a reputation to protect."

With a giggle, I lifted my mouth and received his tongue surging past my lips and stealing my breath from my lungs. He pinned my hips to the tree, stepping between my legs so the fire inside him pressed against my heated core.

The energy between us turned on a dime, shifting from sweet and intimate to hot and passionate. My leg lifted to wrap around his hip and his hand found the flesh of my ass, anchoring me there as he kissed a hot trail down my jaw to my neck.

"Want to call Hunter over here?" I asked, already panting.

"No," he growled, nipping my shoulder. "I want you all to myself right now."

That was the answer I was hoping for. Right then, I didn't want to share my dragon either.

He lowered my leg off him and quickly did away with my shorts, the denim sliding down my bare legs to pool at my feet before I stepped out of them carefully. His throat made a hum of pleasure as he rubbed through my panties, already feeling my wetness through the thin fabric.

I undid his zipper with fumbling hands—too distracted, too noodley with how fucking good he made me feel already. Eventually I pulled him out, only able to stroke his thick, hot shaft for a moment before he pulled my panties aside and shoved into me with one hard thrust.

"Oh... FUCK!"

His cock knocked the breath out of me. It almost bordered on painful as I stretched to accommodate him, his piercings adding even more pressure and sensation I wasn't sure I could handle.

But my dragon lifted both of my legs off the ground and put them around his hips again. Widening my legs gave just a hair of extra room for him to fit. He grinned at my gasp for air, my eyes rolling back in my head as he surged out and then pressed in even deeper. *Good Lord.*

With my ankles locked behind his back and only his cock and impressive strength holding me against the tree, he fucked me with abandon. Gone was my warm, patient teacher. This man was splitting me apart and enjoying it from that wild, hungry look in his eyes.

If I could make sense of anything, I was probably orgasming the entire time he fucked me. My muscles just had no room to convulse and clench, but my clit felt like it was shooting off fireworks the whole time, releasing through my toes, curling so hard my feet cramped. Even my fingertips digging into his shoulders for dear life felt every centimeter of him.

He released with a roar that echoed off the trees, turning his head for a moment to allow a small flame to escape his lips without burning me.

I was covered in sweat. My clothes and bits of tree bark stuck to my skin as he gently lowered my legs to the ground. His slick forehead on mine and his ragged breathing told me the same story. Hot, rough, and probably fast, although I lost all sense of time.

Anyone looking out from the house may have seen us. Or not. I smirked at the thought. It almost felt like having a dirty little secret and I kind of enjoyed that.

No, *really* enjoyed that.

"You're a bad, bad dragon," I teased, pulling my shorts back up my wobbly legs.

"And don't you forget it," he returned with a grin.

❧ 23 ❧

MELODY

"**I**'m so nervous."

"Why?" Raz looked concerned as he helped me out of the truck.

"Just look at this place." My heels clicked and echoed in the parking garage as we walked together to the wall of elevators.

The Vaudeville Theater had loomed up in front of us when we pulled into town—a tall, glitzy building covered in lights and completely unlike the run-down, dirty outdoor carnivals I was used to. The elevator we stepped into, with a plush red carpet and mirrored walls on all sides, reflected that same vibe.

This was a classy establishment, making Money with a capital M. I was so glad Raz and I dressed up for this audition. I wore a classic ringmistress outfit with a red tailcoat and white gloves, plus black tights, heels, a corset, and, of course, a top hat. Raz wore pressed black slacks and shoes, a black button-up shirt with the sleeves rolled to his elbows to show off his tattoos, and a black waistcoat over the top that accentuated his broad chest and tapered waist. In his hand, he carried a slim case for his knives.

"You mean, look at *us*." He slid an arm around my waist, dropping his chin to my shoulder as he stared at our reflection in the mirrored walls. "We look like a million bucks and every bit like we belong here. Don't let anything convince you otherwise, *steluța*."

"I also really want this job," I admitted to our reflections. "I've never stepped on a stage wanting something that I didn't yet have. I actually have to try hard and compete against other people."

"There's no one that holds a candle to you," he murmured with a soft kiss to my neck. "I've seen hundreds of ringmasters and none of them capture an audience like you do. You've got this in the box, *steluța*."

"In the bag, you mean?" I couldn't suppress the giggle that bubbled up.

He looked confused. "Is that what the expression is?"

"Yeah. It's 'you've got this in the bag', not in the box."

"Fucking Arjun," he spat, smiling despite himself. "He taught me English expressions a few years ago, and I knew he was fucking with me on some of them."

The silly moment eased my nerves a bit when we stepped out of the elevator, but my stomach flipped on itself and twisted into knots when the main theater room opened up before us. It was *massive*.

I looked up at a glittering chandelier the size of my old trailer, hung high in the ceiling like it was the sun itself. Two levels of balconies circled around the room, in addition to the many rows of seats here on the ground floor.

A group of acrobats were onstage at the moment, auditioning to four people in the front seats with clipboards.

Raz and I sat down near the back and watched. A girl stood on her hands on a platform, her feet hanging over and down, nearly touching her head. One of the other acrobats finished a floor routine of flips and contortions before grabbing a bow and arrow, tossing both items up to the handstanding girl.

She caught them *with her feet.*

My jaw fell open as she nocked the arrow and pulled the bowstring back taut, all done with her toes. She looked almost bored as the arrow loosed, sailing across the stage to hit the center of a bullseye set up at the other end.

Their music stopped, and all acrobats took a bow, the audition finished. Three of the four people in the audience clapped enthusiastically while the fourth scribbled on the paper attached to her clipboard.

"I think we're next," Razvan muttered as he nudged me.

Fuck. We had to follow *that?*

"Next! Melanie and uh, Rasman?"

"It's Melody," I said through gritted teeth, practically stomping down the aisle to the stage when all I wanted to do was sink into the floor. "And Razvan."

"Right. Take it away, you two. Whenever you're ready."

Raz and I ascended the stage. He shot me a wink before moving behind the curtain, where he'd get my music ready and wait until I called for him to come out. We worked on my announcement after our fun at the tree, then practiced a short routine together. It looked like we'd have to lay all our cards out on the table for tonight.

While waiting for my drumbeat to come over the loudspeaker, I took a better look at the people judging my performance. All of them wore dark suits. A man and woman whispered a soft conversation to each other, then glanced at their watches almost in unison. Great, so they didn't even *want* to be here.

The woman who had been scribbling while the others clapped for the acrobats was a stern-looking blonde with a dark pantsuit and glasses. She was the only one who stared straight up at me, lips pressed thin, and her pen tapping the edge of her clipboard like an impatient teacher. If Arjun thought I had no sense of humor, he would rail on this woman.

Who *were* these people? They all looked so... corporate.

My music started up and my stage smile spread across my face. It felt so natural at this point, like I was a magical doll that the stage and music brought to life.

"Ladies and gentlemen, boys and girls!" I boomed. Despite having no microphone, my voice filled the empty auditorium, even reaching some other auditioners seated in the very back rows. The two people up front whispering to each other even stopped to look at me. "Welcome to the Vaudeville Theater's opening night of our electrifying, heart-pounding, most spectacular special event of the season, A Night in the Jungle!"

I paused dramatically, the two whisperers now on the edges of their seats with their eyes glued to me. The woman in glasses had her eyes on her clipboard and scribbled madly.

"Before we take you through the jungle, dear ladies and gentlemen, we've got to warm you up!" I winked suggestively. "The jungle is dangerous, with animals and traps lurking everywhere, oh my!" My eyes widened as a gloved hand came to my mouth. Gasps elicited from audience members with their eyes glued to me, the woman in glasses scribbling as if nothing at all was being performed in front of her.

"We must arm ourselves to the teeth, boys and girls!" I continued, gnashing my teeth for maximum effect. "We must learn to handle the sweltering heat! Oh!" I held up an index finger, my smile so wide it nearly split my face. "I know just the man to show us the way."

Everyone's eyes followed me hypnotically, their tongues practically wagging as I teased them for the upcoming act. Everyone except Glasses Lady, that is. She finally looked up from her lap and stopped writing, but looked utterly bored.

"From the cold mountains of Romania, this man's fire saved hundreds of villages! He scared away dragons and vampires with his skilled blades! And he's bringing the heat to you now, ladies and gentlemen!" I paused and lowered my voice. "If you can handle him," I added with a wink. Then returning to full volume, "Ladies and gentlemen, boys and girls, I give you the amazing, the stupendous, the most death-defying sword swallower and fire breather in the world, Razvan! Leader of the Flaming Swords!"

Walking off stage, I kept my posture straight and my legs long until I could sit down, where I deflated like a balloon. Damn, it looked easy, but yelling at the top of my lungs plus giving all the right inflections and body language was downright exhausting.

Raz walked out from behind the curtain, a swagger in his shoulders as he juggled knives almost casually.

"Good evening, everyone." His eyes swept across the

panel of judges with a cocky smile, his hands constantly moving.

"Hello!" chirped one of the women in suits with a giggle. I glared daggers at her.

Raz only nodded at her politely as his juggling hands quickly changed their movement.

Tossing all six knives into the air at once, he spread his arms out to the side and leaned his head back. One by one, he caught each blade *in his mouth* as it fell. Screams rang out in the auditorium, much like I did when I first saw the sharp, metal blades fall down his throat. Now it no longer phased me.

"Oh, no!" I said in feigned annoyance, rising from my seat to take my cue. Heads snapped over to look at me as I ascended the stage. "Looks like Raz got the blades stuck again."

I went to him and wrapped my hands around two of the handles resting on his lips, then pantomimed pulling on them as hard as I could.

"Ugh, Raz. You've done it again," I sighed, looking over my shoulder at our dumbfounded audience. "Knife swallowers, am I right?"

Some of them laughed at our exaggerated display, but everyone was still enraptured. At least we still had their attention.

With a final big show of effort, I pulled two knives out of his mouth and pretended to reel back, windmilling my arms from the momentum.

"Ah, glad I got those out!" I wiped my brow. "I didn't want to explain that one again to the people at the hospital."

"The knives! THE KNIVES!" audience members yelled.

"Right? Who sticks knives down their throat for fun?" I asked, pretending to be oblivious to their pointing and shrieking. "This guy, apparently."

"The knives are on fire!"

I looked down at the blades in my hands, now coated with bright, flickering orange flame.

"Aaah!" I shrieked, tossing them in the air just in time for Raz to step up and add them to the four flaming knives he was already juggling.

"Amateur," he teased me with an eye roll. "Don't play with fire unless you can take the heat."

"Oh, yeah?" I shot back flirtatiously. "How much heat can *you* take, Razvan?"

"Hold these and watch."

One by one, he tossed each knife to me, handle first. The flames extinguished before ever reaching me as I fumbled and dropped the still-smoking blades. At least that part wasn't acting.

All eyes on Raz with his hands now free, he pulled two swords from behind his back and proceeded to juggle them, teasing us all for the grand finale.

"Do I have a volunteer?" he called out to the audience.

Several jaws dropped open, including mine, as I stared at him. That was *not* something we rehearsed.

"I'm just kidding," he cracked. "No one come up here. It's extremely dangerous."

It took everything in me to not roll my eyes and slap my forehead. Damn him. Of course he'd do something off-script. Our first kiss was onstage, after all.

More shrieks rang out as fire consumed the sword blades in a slow line from base to tip.

They whirled through the air in a dazzling display, the heat warming my face as he caught and tossed them effortlessly.

"You all might want to stand off to the sides for this," he warned our audience members, who scrambled out of their seats and headed toward the aisles.

He stopped the juggling abruptly, holding each sword out to his sides like some kind of ninja assassin. Then his biceps curled, and he smirked as he tipped his head back, the flaming blades drifting slowly toward his lips.

"No! He's not!"

"Oh, my God! Is he, really?"

He really was.

With slow, careful precision, he lowered the full lengths of the blades down his throat at the same time. I thought the suited people were going to faint. My eyes drifted over to the woman with glasses, who still barely showed any trace of emotion. Her arms were crossed, eyes locked on the dragon shifter, but I couldn't get a read on her at all.

With the swords now fully inserted all the way to his stomach, Raz spread his arms to his sides again and walked forward toward the edge of the stage.

"Holy shit, they're really in there!" someone cried out.

"And he's seriously still alive!"

I saw his chest expand with a breath, knowing what was coming next as he grabbed the handles of the swords sticking out of his mouth. A pause to prepare and then...
ta-da.

He yanked the swords out in one clean pull and

followed the blades with a huge fireball that bathed the whole auditorium in heat.

People ducked and screamed, but it was over. Smirking, he took a bow as I ascended the stage.

"Give it up for Razvan, ladies and gentlemen! Our amazing pyromaniac swordsman!"

Claps and cheers rang out, and I realized more people had come in and caught the end of our audition. The suits up front had tears in their eyes and clapped enthusiastically. Raz wrapped an arm around my waist and we bowed together. He kissed my cheek when we rose and I shot him a stern look that quickly dissolved into a smile. I couldn't be mad at him. He put on an amazing show and stayed somewhat professional, at least.

"Thank you," the woman in glasses muttered, the only one to not clap, as she kept scribbling on that damn clipboard. "NEXT!"

I stood there, stunned, until Raz gently tugged me to leave the stage. That was it?

"Um, will we hear from you?" I asked once I made it to the ground floor. The next act was already shuffling around on stage to prepare.

"We'll give you a call if you're picked," the other suited woman told me with an encouraging smile. "Great job, we just have a lot of auditions to go through."

I nodded, forcing a smile as I waited for Razvan to grab his case from backstage, but as the woman in glasses forgot all about us as she focused on the next audition, my confidence went down like a lead balloon.

✤ 24 ✤

MELODY

I felt like an utter failure as we left, despite Raz trying his best to cheer me up.

"They can't show any preference when watching a ton of auditions like that," he told me, rubbing a sympathetic hand over my thigh as he drove. "It'll make everyone else not want to try."

"I've never seen anyone watch a performance so coldly, with no reaction at all," I mumbled, thoroughly puzzled by the woman in glasses.

"Yeah, she was a real stick in the mud, ah?" he agreed. "Made it feel like a real job interview. Maybe she represented investors or something, and all she was concerned about was how much we'd bring in. Fuck knows what kind of money goes into a place like that."

"On the bright side," I leaned against his shoulder, eager for a happier topic, "I didn't sense a single shifter in there. Did you?"

"Nope." He planted a kiss on my forehead. "You were

really feeling for them? Good girl. I didn't even notice you trying."

"I've been practicing a little," I admitted. "At home, I try to identify the differences between you, Hunter, the pups, and Arjun. I can do it pretty much constantly now without thinking too much. It's like feeling different currents in the air. Hunter is a cool breeze. The pups are like little gusts of wind, probably because of how rambunctious and playful they are."

"What about me and the kitty?" he teased, squeezing his hand around my knee.

"You're always warm," I answered. "I think depending on your mood, you feel like a warm blanket or a scorching hot desert."

"Scorching. I like that," he chuckled. "And Arjun?"

I took a moment to think, trying to accurately describe the enigmatic tiger with shifting blue-green eyes.

"He's like the rush of air going past you in a car, or a rollercoaster." I rolled down the window and stuck my hand out. Yes, sensing Arjun's presence felt a lot like the air rushing between my fingers. "It's always fast-moving and a possible indication of danger."

"He would never hurt you, you know," Raz glanced at me before returning his eyes to the road. "That wasn't the first human he killed, but he's only ever attacked the ones who actively enjoyed harming us. He's a predator. It's in his DNA, but that means he only kills to eat or to survive."

"I know that," I replied. "When I sense him, it's not danger like that. It's more of a rush, a thrill. A rollercoaster like I said, or going over the speed limit."

"Ah, so he's another bad boy for ya," he teased,

grinning.

"No way!" I protested, slapping his shoulder. "You're plenty bad enough for me. I'm still sore from earlier today, by the way."

"That's what I like to hear," he crooned.

We made it home as the sun was setting and shadows grew long. The truck wound down the long driveway to the house, where two small, fuzzy figures raced around the lawn at top speed. Hunter burst out onto the porch just as we pulled up, yelling at Roo and Rinna for shifting where humans could possibly see. I smiled as I unbuckled my seatbelt and slid out of the car. Home sweet home.

"How'd it go?" Hunter asked, holding a squirming half-shifted Rinna under his arm. She finally wriggled out then tore off after Roo, finishing her shift back to wolf with high-pitched puppy barks.

"Okay, I think," I muttered, approaching my tall, sexy wolf. I missed him. It felt so long since I had any alone time with him now.

"Just okay?" He pulled me into his arms, brow furrowed with concern, as he gave me a kiss. I clung to him, deepening the kiss when he tried to pull back, wanting to forget all about the audition and just curl up into him.

"She did amazing. They were going through a lot of auditions in a short time, so we didn't get any feedback either way," Raz explained. "Just said they'll call if we're picked."

"You did amazing." I looked over my shoulder at him. "It was your act, really. I was just an accessory."

"Not true, *steluţa*. You set the scene, I just followed and did my part."

"I'm sure they'll call. Go on inside," Hunter swatted my ass. "Arjun has a surprise for you."

"Arjun... what?" My brain couldn't make sense of those words. They did not compute.

"Go on. You'll see," Hunter grinned.

"Great," I muttered, dragging my feet up the porch. What could this possibly be?

Not at all eager to find out what the cheeky tiger had in store for me, I hesitated and looked over my shoulder. Hunter approached Raz, their faces close together and talking in low voices I couldn't hear. Raz's hand then shot out and grabbed a fistful of Hunter's hair close to his scalp. He pulled the wolf's mouth to his, closing the already narrow distance for a rough, hot kiss full of teeth and tongue.

Heat burned in my belly as I watched them. Hunter grabbed the sides of Raz's waist and yanked him even closer, their strong, masculine bodies flush against each other. They were rougher with each other than with me, and that only made me hotter.

Raz opened one steel-gray eye, catching my gaze over Hunter's shoulder. His lips pulled back in a grin, breaking off the kiss with the wolf.

"Can a dragon and a wolf get some privacy from perving eyes?" he teased.

Hunter turned around and made a shooing motion at me before Raz grabbed the back of his neck and directed his attention back to where it belonged, at least for that moment.

I giggled as I made my way up the porch, realizing I loved that I wouldn't be the only one sharing lovers. If anything, it made things easier. When those two were together, I could have alone time with Connor, or get to know the kids better. And then Raz or Hunter could have some space when one of them was with me.

And when all of us are together...

My mind remained firmly in a naughty daydream until I walked through the kitchen, and then the smell made my mouth water.

"What is that?" I sniffed the air, unfamiliar with it but unable to deny the growling hunger in my stomach.

"It's curry." Arjun turned from the stove, slapping a dish towel over his shoulder. "Come here, have a taste."

I narrowed my eyes suspiciously but approached him anyway, my curiosity and hunger getting the better of me.

He held out a spoon with a steaming yellowish-green sauce with flecks of spices, herbs, and whatever else was in there. I blew the steam away first, then accepted a small taste.

"Wow!" My eyes widened with the flavors exploding on my tongue. Savory, creamy, a little sweet, and a whole smorgasbord of unique spices and tastes I'd never experienced in my life before. "That is," I licked my lips, "so freaking good!"

"I didn't want to go too exotic on your bland American palate so I kept the heat down and made it with chicken instead of lamb."

I looked at him, those green-blue eyes still mischievous and full of cheek but no outright hostility. His entire demeanor was more relaxed and open than I'd seen before.

"You made this for me?" I asked, dumbfounded.

"Well, for all of us, but I wanted you to experience it, yes," he answered. "You need some culture if we're going to tolerate each other in the same household."

I rolled my eyes at that, but I could see the effort he was making. This curry was an olive branch. Not necessarily an apology for being a dick earlier, but he was making an effort to understand me, to meet me halfway. And this was simple proof he wasn't above being nice once in a while.

"Well, thank you. It's delicious." I offered him a smile. "You're going to give Hunter some serious competition in the kitchen."

"Eh, don't get too used to it," he muttered, returning his attention to the simmering sauce on the stove. "I've got simple tastes myself. A good curry is a bit labor-intensive and you've got to get all the ingredients just right. I'm content with a sausage roll and a spot of tea, myself." He shot me a dazzling white smile that threatened to send my heartbeat out of rhythm.

Thankfully, Connor wheeled in right then.

"Smells amazing, RJ. Let's all eat outside, the sunset's fucking gorgeous. Hey babe, how'd the audition go?"

He tilted his head up for a kiss, which I gave to him long and slow. "It was okay. I'll tell you about it later," I murmured, resting my forehead on his. "Also, RJ?"

"Don't ask me," Arjun said, pulling bowls down from the cupboards. "No point in a fuckin' nickname if it's got the same amount of syllables as my real name."

"It rolls off the tongue easier," Connor chuckled with a swat to my hip. "Help me set up outside, babe."

"Sure it does, with a thick American tongue like you've got."

"That's what she said!" Connor cackled, rolling through the house while balancing bowls on his lap.

"Not like that. Thick means... nevermind."

I giggled, carrying the large bowl of rice out to the back deck while Arjun followed me with the pot of curry.

"Thanks, Mel," he said when I held the door open for him.

"You're welcome, RJ." I couldn't help it.

"Bloody hell. Not you too," he groaned, but a smirk escaped as he placed the still simmering pot on the patio table.

Hunter and Raz finished their make-out session in the front yard and came around to join us. Roo and Rinna sat still enough to eat a small bowl of curry with rice each before running off to chase each other and wrestle again.

"They love the open space," Connor smiled as he watched the pups play.

"It's good for them to get their energy out," Hunter agreed, leaning back from his empty bowl. "I hated keeping them cooped up in the den back in Crying Falls. At least here I know they're safe."

We all chatted and ate like a normal family as the sun went down. I went back for seconds on the curry and almost considered getting thirds, but my belly was thoroughly stuffed as I sat back and rubbed a hand over it.

"Aw, my babe has a food baby," Connor teased as he rubbed a hand over me as well. I slapped his hand away, laughing. That was when it hit me like a bucket of ice water to the face.

We didn't use a condom last time.

No one seemed to notice me freeze up, and I exhaled the breath I held, trying to calm down. I'd have to talk to him about it later when we were alone. When did it happen? Two days ago? Hopefully, it wasn't too late to take Plan B, nor was it too hard to get it somewhere nearby.

It's probably nothing to worry about. I've had a few scares before, but nothing came of them.

Connor suddenly waved a hand to quiet everyone's conversations, bringing a finger to his lips and shushing loudly.

"Do y'all hear that?" he whispered.

Silence fell over the table. No one moved a muscle until we heard the faint, eerie sounds of howling. Goosebumps erected over my skin despite the warm air. The song was haunting, sad, and beautiful.

"Wolves here?" Connor whispered. "Man, I never—"

"Shh!" He was abruptly cut off by Hunter, whose brow furrowed as he listened hard. Then his eyes widened in shock. Color drained from his face as his mouth opened. "My god, there's no way. It can't be—"

He was drowned out by the sounds of Roo and Rinna, suddenly yipping and howling back with frenzied excitement. Roo quickly shifted to human, jumping up and down like it was Christmas morning.

"Dad, it's Uncle Colt and Uncle Gabe!" he shrieked. Rinna already ran toward the treeline and Roo shifted back and sped off after her, answering the wolf howls with his own.

"Hunter?" Raz elbowed the pale wolf, who still appeared to be in shock. "Who's out there?"

"Their uncles. My brothers," Hunter whispered. "My pack is here."

Thank you so much for reading Jump Through Fire! Book 5 in the series, ***Tightrope, is available now!***

AUTHOR'S NOTE

Dear reader,

Thank you for coming this far with me on Mel and her boys' rollercoaster ride! I hope you've been enjoying the twists and turns, the highs and the lows. Tightrope will release in February 2019, followed by Curtain Call in March, which will mark the end of the series.

We're over halfway there now, but I've still got lots to throw at these characters! As someone wiser than me said, it ain't over 'til it's over.

See you soon!

Crystal

NEWSLETTER & READER GROUP

Never miss a book release, plus get three *free* short stories when you sign up for my newsletter!

Grab your freebies at:
crystalashbooks.com/freebies

You can also join my reader group on Facebook to get updates and hang out with fellow readers.

Join Crystal's Coven at:
facebook.com/groups/crystalscoven

ABOUT THE AUTHOR

Crystal Ash is a USA Today Bestselling Author from California. She loves writing steamy, heart-wrenching romance with tortured heroes, especially if they're in a reverse harem. Crystal's other loves include animals, mythology, and well-crafted alcohol, most of which can also be found in her stories.

When she's not writing, she's probably drinking craft beer with her husband or trying to coax her feral cat into accepting affection.

crystalashbooks.com

facebook.com/Crystal.Ash.Romance

instagram.com/crystalashbooks

amazon.com/author/crystalash

bookbub.com/profile/crystal-ash